TONY MERINO

UNCHOSEN

Copyright © 2024 by Tony Merino

All rights reserved. No part of this publication may be reproduced, stored or transmitted in any form or by any means, electronic, mechanical, photocopying, recording, scanning, or otherwise without written permission from the publisher. It is illegal to copy this book, post it to a website, or distribute it by any other means without permission.

This novel is entirely a work of fiction. The names, characters and incidents portrayed in it are the work of the author's imagination. Any resemblance to actual persons, living or dead, events or localities is entirely coincidental.

Tony Merino asserts the moral right to be identified as the author of this work.

First edition

This book was professionally typeset on Reedsy. Find out more at reedsy.com

To Mom and Dad, my proofreader Rossana and my book cover artist Cristina. This book would not exist without you all. What a wonderful gaggle of silly gooses... who all need therapy.

"We are all in the gutter, but some of us are looking at the stars."

-Oscar Wilde

Contents

1	"SHIT"	1
2	"Meanwhile at Zigma 4226"	10
3	"Ted Coalboar"	13
4	"Uli Einsworth"	15
5	"The Sword, The Witch and the Redhead"	20
6	"Late"	22
7	"Disturbance in the course"	31
8	"President Volshtadt"	34
9	"Scatter Lands"	40
10	"Auntie Ogun"	45
11	"Welcome to the light show"	51
12	"Blood Fucker is bored"	60
13	"Gunther and Olaff"	71
14	"Silent Ride"	74
15	"Secrets"	78
16	"Luminous Lakes Mall"	83
17	"Tomb Sniffer"	87
18	"Carl Weatherson"	92
19	"Hot on the trail"	98
20	"The Near Infinite Staircase to the dead guy who's gonna...	101
21	"Mr. Sundae"	119
22	"The Weatherson Stronghold"	123
23	"Devil is in the Detail"	129

24	"Sort of Ranger Carl"	140
25	"Dinner Party"	145
26	"About Last Night"	156
27	"Black Forest Jam"	166
28	"Burn The Rich"	170
29	"Hiking in Hell"	174
30	"Decay"	180
31	"Tag Team"	188
32	"Stranger Ranger Danger"	191
33	"A Lazy Escape"	204
34	"Forest Fighting"	211
35	"And Then There Were Three-ish"	224
36	"House Party"	227
37	"Unrest In Peace"	244
38	"Chosen One"	249
39	"Stumped"	256
40	"Panicked Room"	261
41	"Magic Cows"	263
About the Author		267

1

"SHIT"

When a warrior, wizard or king loses their life in battle, their bowels rid them of any dignity by further soiling the blood soaked battleground. So yeah… they shit themselves.

At the hollowed stones of the Alzahar Crater, anything with a pulse was dispensing their last loaf as they died in glorious combat, the prize being the control of the planet known as Thira.

Either good prevailed, thus consolidating a millennia of peace and prosperity. Or darkness does its thing and the world is thrown into a hell pit of despair where death is the nice ending.

And in this particular cycle of life, the one up to bat for the baddies was the one known as DARK LORD VOLSHTADT.

For fourteen weeks, the battle cries and death rattles of the Millithid Coalition crashed against the hellion hoards of Volshtadt.

Eight feet tall, pale as moonlight, hair of bantam black. If the embodiment of death took up a modeling career, it would be the ugly understudy to the gothic monolith that is Volshtadt! Tamer of the abyss!

The corrupt mages of the Forlen coast whipped up a conception ritual most vile and filthy, charged with every incantation of every grimoire penned by the most sadistic of warlocks. A two day orgy/ritual involving mages, dragons and random barnyard animals, wallowing in pit of depravity. Any who bore witness felt compelled to rip their eyes out at the horrors that spawned the dark champion.

The messed up freak fest birthed a being impervious to any blade or spell. All fear, doubt and flaw was eugenically eradicated from this big boy of blasphemy, leaving a being of perfect cunning, bred for one purpose alone...

Victory by means of ultra violence.

To counteract this agent of doom, the oracles of Millithid listened to the prophetic songs whispered by the omniscient cosmos. The rather repetitive melody sang as follows...

"From hand of chosen man, shall the Dammerung slay the dark lord's command!"

World class record selling lyricist the Omniscient Cosmos was not. But it got the point through and understood easily enough.

The holiest of holy swords, Dammerung compressed the infinite power of a dimension of pure light into the only weapon capable of killing even the most powerful Kings of evil.

Aiden Pollthic, raised by the Druid Nomad Clans of the

northeastern plains, was the one who would charge against said darkness. His people murdered by Volshtadt's draconic guard. The poor boy drifted into the emerald harbor using a very unique flotation device, the Dammerung Blade.

Aiden grew into a behemoth of a man, eyes of auburn, hair so blond, the only thing more golden was his heart. He trained with the warrior mages of Millithid, honing his vengeance into a weapon as powerful as the holy sword that glowed in his hands. He etched into the blade the name of every soul slain in his clan, so when it found its final home in Volshtadt's chest, his people would taste the demise of the one who took them from him.

Volshtadt's army stood back as the Voidlord took the vanguard. They witnessed in silent awe the devastation their king could bring forth with a single swing of his demonic greatsword known as Thigg.

Cyclones of black flame exploded from his cursed sword, cutting platoons of men into nothing but feed for the carrion crows that hovered around the carnage. The dark one's demeanor was that of a predator lost in the ecstasy of the hunt, and he was soon to run out of sheep.

The thundering gallop of a single horse cut the horrid sounds of the one sided bloodbath. Every god, demon and supernatural whatchamacallit tuned in to bear witness to this moment in history, the crescendo of war was getting to it's climax, and the powers that be were ready for the money shot.

Riding his snow stallion Hillios, Aiden charged through, vivisecting the hoards of Volshtadt with every plasma flared slash. Dammerung's edge cut through the night sky with such radiance you would have thought the sword commanded the very sun to break into the war scarred canyon.

Aiden became a beacon to his men. Force feeding their hopes and dreams into his incandescent weapon of fate, rendering it brighter and brighter, blinding all with his blade's holy light.

In that moment, Volshtadt had his brain pierced by something far sharper than the very sword Aiden wanted to stab him with, fear!

Every hair, every cell, every atom within him shivered with the instinctual need to get the fuck out of there.

But, like I said, it was really, REALLY bright...

And I don't know when was the last time you stepped into a war zone. But good vision is an important thing to have in such an event.

This is where the "Shit" of it all comes into play. All that fallen soldier excrement made the hard gritted grounds of Alzahar as slippery as a fish with a petroleum jelly fetish.

Volshtadt was ready to clash with his fated foe and meet his destiny. But Hillios, that poor horse, never before had its hooves defiled by the putrid presence of warrior dung. So when the post mortem dump of one Private Edgar Weatherson lubed up the floor. The elegant equine's front right hoof gave into the slickness.

Hellios' ankle popped, its pain paralyzed body crashed into soiled terrain, causing the horse to turn into a very powerful organic catapult, thus hurling the chosen one straight into the

"SHIT"

Lord of Despair! (yes, he does have a large amount of titles and nicknames, good for you for noticing).

Ever the resourceful hero, Aiden took the moment into his favor and readied his dimensional sword for a god killing strike, shaping his very destiny into a projectile of justice aimed dead center at the murderer of all he loved and cherished.

But the stirrup, that damned left stirrup.

The gaudy garbage snagged Aiden's foot, redirecting Aiden into a half mooned body slam on the craggy ground. What busted his mortal coil was his twelve hundred pound horse falling on top of his spine, instantly breaking it, as well as pulverizing his ribs, collapsing his lungs, and crushing his heart to a fine paste.

The blade's radiance flickered away to pale muted reality, bringing the battlefield back into the embrace of night. Signaling with its dying splendor the end of the war. Not with the epic contest of good vs. evil. Not with heroic sacrifices that would inspire many a bard towards somber songs, nope.

A horse slid on some shit and broke the chosen one's body like a sun baked chicken carcass.

It took Volshtadt a moment to process all that had transpired.

His fate appointed rival, dead.

The sanguine armies of Forlen victorious. The evil king turned his gaze to the one half of the prophecy that could still end him, that light show of a sword, Dammerung. Its brilliance wept with the sentient need to rid the world of the

Voidlord.

Volshtadt needed it gone. His armored boot crashed upon the flat of the blade, every earth shattering strike leaving nothing but scratches. He brought to force his famed gravity magic, mountains and meteors crashed down in an effort to fulminate the blade. The ludicrous display of space shattering magic only sharpened its edge. He summoned the world ending fires of the primeval dragon *Lumithix*. The colossal city scorching reptile couldn't even peel the cerulean paint within the cross guard.

Volshtadt roared with such ear piercing power it ripped a hole in the cloud covered chasm the size of Alzahar crater itself. The star covered night sky gave him an idea worthy of his ludicrous power.

"Exile it is then!"

His right hand boiled and charred as he gripped the condensed antithesis to his existence that was the Dammerung. He channeled his pain and rage into launching the accursed thing into the one place it could never come back from, outer space.

It broke the sound barrier as it ripped through the atmosphere. Both armies of the concluded battle looked at it go, and they all had the same question, "What the fuck now?"
    The pillars of destiny, fate and causality collapsed into uncertainty the further Dammerung exited their particular sector of the galaxy.
    The rule of Lord Volshtadt was about to swallow up Thira.

"SHIT"

And the only one who had any idea on what to do, was the very figurehead of the Forlen Warlocks responsible for Volshtadt's creation, the big brain wicked codger known as Kalammet Vinmoth.

A few of the remaining faithful tried to avenge the (accidental) death of the druid prince. but any flame of rebellion was snuffed out with ruthless efficiency. As for the rest of the world, submit or die was the operating policy.

From the icy peaks of the Zorbok mountains, to the mystical sand dunes of Voran Sammat. The kingdoms of man were swept with an instinctual reflex of bending the knee, all in the name of survival. The whole "Cities on fire while every man, woman and child are put to shackles and forced to pick whole mountains bare till they die of exhaustion and/or black lung" was the expected future. All while Volshtadt and company fed on virgins while swimming in baby unicorn blood.

And yes, The big bad men with blood drenched banners did march into every town and city they found. But no heads were chopped, no women kidnapped, quite the opposite.

They went to every home, shop and brothel with a rather comprehensive census on how to optimize the machinations of each part of the many kingdoms toward the unified glory of the Forlen Empire.

Volshtadt's intellect was only rivaled by the combined brain power of the wizards that brought him to be. But both he and his head wizard Kalammet's true power existed in their ability for foresight.

They saw that the whole doom and gloom approach to world domination was not sustainable in the long run. You force the faces of millions into the fires, sooner or later a few hundred thousand of them would try to jump start an insurrection. This had to be done with the long game in mind. You can't get rid of free will in one fell swoop, it has to be dripped away, slowly, methodically, so the backwater ingrates you take it from don't even notice its gone.

Generation after generation was born, used up and put in the ground, with each century the world slowly forgetting the past, history books altered one word at a time in favor to Volshtadt, so on and so forth until such historically pertinent moments in the history of Thira was treated more like myth than fact.

Gone were the records of Prince Aiden. Gone were the songs and legends regarding all the mystical things that gave Thira its natural sense of wonder. And wonder dear reader is one of the most powerful forces in any reality, and Kalammet's plan required a members only access to such a potent resource.

Technology had its place in the subjugation of it all. Every decade or so someone developed a new form of transportation, a new kitchen appliance or some novel brain dulling entertainment, all of them curated by Kalammet towards making loyal subjects to Volshtadt more malleable, compliant and dull.

Civil wars came and went, a plague or two did their viral murder spree. But for the most part, Thira kept on turning.

But at the end of the day you still had to wake up, go to work, pay your part, and lose a gram of your soul every start of the work week.

Control is not about making your sheep tremble as they walk into the meat grinder. It's about dumbing them down enough to think that the meat grinder has free cable and orgasm inducing donuts.

Many a thousand years later, Thira looked very much like the Earth you folks have. Motor vehicles, digital entertainment, booze, porn, all the pillars of modern civilization.

Every technological step fading the presence of magic further and further away from humanity. No need to learn the ancient ways of pyromancy to get a fire going when the electric stove blazes away at the flick of a switch. Why dabble in alchemy when the pharmacy has the painkillers on special every Monday.

Magic was wild and unruly, science could be molded and controlled to the whims of Volshtadt and the grand council under him.

Few outside of "President" Volshtadt and his council still practiced the arcane ways in secret, keeping some of the ancient traditions alive. If any regular civilian was ratted out by their neighbors for using magic, these unlucky ones were sent to "reeducation" camps, rarely to be seen again.

So the bad guys won, Volshtadt's grip on humanity consolidated with Kalammet's perfected sedation of the masses and Thira has never been more in order, yet more miserable than ever.

Order is a fortress, forever burdened to build a taller wall to keep chaos at bay, but if you erect it too tall and narrow, any idiot can topple it over.

In this case, two idiots.

2

"Meanwhile at Zigma 4226"

The inhabitants of ZIGMA 4226 are a gelatinous folk, they danced and jiggled as they kicked off their spring festival. Said annual tradition was brought to an abrupt stop when a certain space exiled sword crash landed in the middle of its capital, right on top of their illustrious leader President Filliquill, destroying with him the once great city of GOMA 5. Its long blade towered over the translucent jelly people like a terrifying harbinger of death, being thirty two *gooznats* taller than their biggest skyscraper. Two weeks it took for the dust to settle around Dammerung, bringing with its arrival death, blood and dozens of questions.

The two main faiths of Zigma, The Church of OOM and their religious rivals the Family of the Thenagen Suns, could not come to an agreement on which one of their one true creators sent this doomsday monolith to their peaceful planet.

The Oomenites thought Dammerung a broken piece of the Great Oom's coral crown, heralding his second coming to save them from the barbarian faiths of the lower born people of Zigma.

But the Thenegans believed it to be an omen for the "Great swallowing," In which the three suns melded together and ate every last jelly person on the planet, bringing on a new age were the pious and humble will evaporate and become one with Thenag, becoming lubricant for his great mating with the mother of creation, thus birthing forth Zigma 4227, (Thenegan church going involved a lot of amorphous sex positive activities, such as "Splitting the pool pony" and "The raxian back blender bender.")

Things took a dark turn when the Thenegans took it as an act of aggression to their sun god when the Oomen faith tried to smelt the entire sword with the intent to fashion a new crown for their soon to arrive god king.

Assumptions made, mistakes perpetrated, and a few dozen political assassinations gave forth to a two millennia spanning holy war coined amongst the Zigma archivists as the Suncrown war.

As to not overwhelm you with this interplanetary tangent, I will hit you with the top historical talking points of the whole misguided affair.

-The Ooman burning of the hive crops of sector eight. The whole planet smelled of fresh baked cookies for a year.

-The black hole bomb, imploding the floating temples of Oom.

- As to extend collective olive branches, an interfaith wedding between twenty thousand of each faith's most devoted followers turned into the bloodiest battle in the history of the conflict.

-And the one year peace treaty caused by local pop star Ninfa Prime releasing her third album "Nibble my jiggle bits

Vol. 2."

Millions perished, countries destroyed, all was lost. The dwindling remnants of the squishy people of Zigma banded together to stop this useless bloodshed once and for all. The great engineers and scholars fused together to concoct the blueprints for a "Quantum Launcher," an apparatus strong enough to slingshot the unwanted sword off their war torn planet.

And on Linquith the 8th, standard sea rim time, The end of the Suncrown war was consolidated with the launching of Dammerung back into the blackness of space, onto its millennia spanning trek through the lonely corners of the galaxy to be forgotten by the People of Thira and Zigma 4226 for all eternity.

Call it fate, luck, or how the grand gears of cosmic happenstance perpetuate their nonsense. But the king killing greatsword shot its way back to the one place it never thought to see again, Thira.

Smack dab on Ted's car.

3

"Ted Coalboar"

Nestled well within the heartland of Thira's rural communities was a solitary motorhome, devoid of wheels and decorated with a lovely layer of rust and lead paint.

Several feet away from said home stood Ted Coalboar, mouth agape and wearing most of his coffee on his shirt. The six foot three, red headed twenty-something stood paralyzed as he beheld the crater the U.F.O made crash landing on the only property to his name, his beloved 550 spearfish sedan.

The shell shock allowed only one thought to solidify in his hungover brain.

"Imma be late for work."

Ted reasoned that the universe usually enjoys ruining your life in threes.

First with his girlfriend commemorating their three year anniversary by breaking up with him. The locally loved Becky Kormen enjoyed Ted's company, she just couldn't wrap herself around the whole walk not run, routine is peace, pussy ass bullshit vibe Ted had been throwing out lately.

The second cosmic kick in the shins came from his current place of employment, the family friendly franchise globally known by its catchy name "Findar's Pizza Emporium and Pasta Barn," where his job bussing tables was now on the thinnest of ice.

"Mark" the teenage manager, made it clear to the ginger giant that his performance was not up to snuff with the powerful, peppy presence the Findar's staff was famous for, and if he didn't put some gusto and muscle Into it, they were going to have to let him go.

And the third spot on the bad luck list goes to the middle finger that came from outer space and destroyed his beloved jalopy.

Ted hoped this trinity of nut shots was the end of it. He rubbed his eyes and sighed, he needed a ride, and the only person strange enough, crazy enough, and bored enough to be his friend was his only option, he just wasn't sure he could handle that particular morning the cyclone of positive energy that is the tiny terror he knows as Uli Einsworth.

4

"Uli Einsworth"

Uli was in her dungeon/laboratory, or what her parents and the rest of Thira would call a basement. She was busy conducting one of her rituals.

Uli is the last "living" Necromancer in the Forlen controlled empires.

Twenty years old, five feet tall, whiter than a bleached albino dove, and dressing like a goth punk princess that also secretly wants a heart covered pink unicorn for her birthday. The embodiment of contrast, thanks to the fact that she dabbles in the long dead magic of undead manipulation, but also having the necessity to inject maximum sunshine into everyone she comes into contact with, rather they like it or not.

And next in line about to endure her positivity, was a dead squirrel she picked up from the service road near her house. The woodland creature was splayed out within a circle made of chalk, her father's hobby table serving as the altar, the poor little fellow still had the tire marks tattooed on his torso.

She opened a raggedy notebook titled "Uli's unholy grimoire of power," jotted on its sticker drowned cover. Flash cards and doodles filled every page of her home made spell book, all of it the result of Uli's many years researching magic, which I remind you has been rendered illegal.

She pricked her thumb with a replica of a ceremonial knife she got from crazy aunt Ogun, dropped a bit of blood into the mouth of the fluffy tailed roadkill, purple wisps of luminous energy twirled around the squirrel.

Uli had done this ritual dozens of times, mostly with recently poisoned household roaches, all of them surviving no more than ten seconds before they exploded.

Since discovered, her necromantic powers could only muster up enough mojo to reanimate the most minuscule of critters. But the air that morning felt thick with energy, like a house full of muted televisions, you can't hear anything, but you can feel them radiating all around you.

"By the words and ways of the land of the dead! The Umbral Mog! I bind your soul to mine, your life is now an extension of my own! Rise forth and curse the floor you walk on, for your life is an affront to the laws of man and gods! I claim the key! And the key's name is *UMBRA SINTAROS!*"

Purple wind manifested shooting into every orifice the squirrel had. Bones cracked into place, oxygen pumped into his tiny rotten lungs. Putrid, corrosive bile shot out its snout, landing on Papa's favorite workbench, the caustic acid boring holes into the iron oak table. Bat wings much too small for any level of flight sprouted from his back. To make his demonic visage complete, two horns popped up between his ears.

Dead black eyes glowed with living intent, he has risen! The little guy ran around the basement with the reanimated delight only the recently revived will ever enjoy. "Who am I? What am I? Who is this big white lady with too much eyeliner?" questions the squirrel felt jumping all over his thimble sized brain, but quickly forgot, for this was a time for celebration, not investigation.

Uli wiped away a tar like liquid from her lower lip, the sour tones in its flavor now more akin to freshly burnt charcoal, her momentary loss of balance reminding her of the price of forging a spell, this dizzy spell was known in certain circles as the rebound, think of it as a instant hangover from dabbling with the dark arts.

After squeaking and tweaking around Uli's' well worn platform boots, the acorn munching minion clawed up its new master and perched himself on her shoulder. From the moment he came back online, he felt this ever present need to be close to this lady. As if imprinting through a twisted version of rebirth. Whatever the case, he felt a kinship with the pale human who brought him back.

"You need a name little guy?"

"Squeak squeak," said the squirrel with a "No shit lady!" tone to it.

She knew exactly what name to give whatever critter ended up being her magical assistant. It was the name of the lead singer of her favorite Death Punk Reggae band Midnight Murder Beach. She gazed into the adorable eyes of her new pet, scratching lovingly under his white tipped chin.

"Your name is…BLOOD FUCKER."

Blood Fucker flicked his ears back and forth and went flag pole straight, he crawled all around her getting an undead case of the zoomies, "I guess you like it!"

Uli laughed with maniacal triumph, eyes wide and wild with adrenaline of a spell gone right. Blood Fucker joined in with his own rendition of sidekick snickers.

"First roadkill! Then an army of undead demon dogs!" Uli said with the chest puffing bravado of a newly minted dictator, "I'll wear those cloaks with the super big shoulder pads, and tiaras made out of finger bones! Oh! And bring back gam gam and ask if she actually killed grams! Awesome!"

The rudest phone on Thira interrupted her brainstorming session with a sonic assault of panicked bell rattles. "Could someone pick that up please!?" She said with frustration laced with politeness.

BLILILILILING! "Oh balls," the moment spoiled by modern technology, she placed Blood Fucker back on the bench and power stomped her way up the stairs to the cutest white and light blue tiled decorated cottage style kitchen you can ever imagine, the amount of recycled wood and Whimsy was enough to make even the most hardened of criminal crave baking peanut brittle and sipping lavender tea.

She picked up the wall mounted phone.

"Good morning! Einsworth residence. Uli speaking, how can I help you?"

"Your polite voice still scares me." Ted said.

Uli's proper operator persona faded fast, morphing into a genuine smirk that only the mightiest of best friends can cause.

"Shut up, Shouldn't you be at Pasta Barn by now?"

"Should be but cant, need a ride, come get me please," Ted

said, stretching out the the "please" as annoyingly possible.

"What happened to Chubbs, the immortal machine!?" She said, while eyeballing a giant batch of cookies her mom just baked, elegantly displayed on one of the good plates, with a note leaning on them that reads "For guests later today! Only take two. Love mama bear."

Uli swiped two chocolate chips and one oatmeal, she's a rebel not a jerk. And Mama bear knows that too, so she secretly made three for Uli anyways.

She asked her cautious compadre what had happened to Ted's noble steed.

All he muttered was "A space sword killed my Chubby boy."

"I'll be right there!" she dry gulped a cookie and hung up.

She went for Blood Fucker and her spell book, stuffing both into her black worn leather satchel.

She raised the garage door and cranked to life her 4150 lime green Equinaut, the former Einsworth Family station wagon, Now Uli's gas guzzling hand me down. She punched it out of the driveway, burning her bald tires at the ludicrous speed of 25 miles per hour, just to gaze upon the possibility of something she's been wishing for her whole life.

A call to adventure!

5

"The Sword, The Witch and the Redhead"

Uli ran around the crater for two minutes. Ted expected this reaction, but the man was minutes away from being late.

"I know right? Crazy, anywho, how about that ride to work?" urgency peppering every syllable.

Uli slid down to the remains of Chubbs the car.

"Hey! Hey no wait dammit! Take me to work and you can come back and play with the damn thing all you want," Ted said, Uli ran her fingers across the rust covered weapon, catching glimpses of its splendor between the crusted up coat of film leftover from Zigma 4226, and the miscellaneous particles of space dust.

"Uli, come on! Mark will have my ass if I don't make it." Uli didn't bother looking at him,

"Uli please, Just drop me off and..." Uli launched her keys at Ted's hard to miss forehead.

"OW!" Ted bellowed.

"Take the car."

"You know I can't drive your car! It has all those tricks to keep it running and stuff," Ted said.

"You mean stick shift?"

Ted said nothing for a beat and looked embarrassed, "Yeah."

"Fine, help me put it in the car and I'll drive you to work." Uli said.

"Fuck that! I have to leave that there to show to the insurance company, maybe I can get some money from it at least."

"Don't think insurance covers swords from the sky buddy."

"You don't know that!" Ted whined.

"Did you even pay your insurance?" asked Uli. Ted was about to bark a retort before his mind realized why he had an extra fifty Voldic dollars last month for no reason.

Uli tried picking up the sword, but twenty years of successfully avoiding the gym resulted with her not budging the space crap covered giant.

"Time's a wastin big guy, either chuck this in the wagon, or your ass is getting the boot on the poop."

Ted wanted to poop boot Uli at the moment. But desperation and the idea of no job make Ted a very obedient boy.

He hauled his con-woman of a friend out of the hole and jumped in to pick up the sword that killed Chubbs the car.

6

"Late"

The tip of the sword poked out of the station wagon's rolled down trunk window, Uli's old plaid shirts served as cushions so as to not further damage the bruised but not busted beloved car.

Ted sat a grumpy Gus as he noticed out the passenger window Mr. Handrax's cloud cows (coined the cute term due to their cloud shaped spots) munching away at the infinite salad bar that was kind Mr. Handrax's farm. Ted looked at them with envy, they didn't have his troubles, they just stood around eating grass and got their nipples sucked by milk pumps all day. The only thing sucking hard at the moment was Ted's life, but at least he had company, annoying, loud, obnoxious company that can drive a stick shift.

"Best day ever!" Uli exclaimed as she looked at the sword and not the road, "A huge ass sword!"

"Yup," Ted answered despondently.

"From space!"

"Uh huh..."

"Murdered your car! This is a sign, I know it!"

Ted's face contorted in disgust to the statement.

"It's not a sign."

"Yeah huh it is…"

"No huh, probably dropped from a plane, or helicopter or something like that."

"You said space, no take backsies, it's from space, I just know It!"

"It's a cosmic middle finger to my life is what it is!"

"Not only is it a sign, It's a call to adventure!" Uli said.

"I don't need swords, and fates, and, and, calls to adventure right now! I need to get my house in order!"

"Why? Are you like, dying? Oh! Maybe I can revive you now too!"

Ted closed his eyes, exhausted from being swallowed by the snowball of bullshit he was now a part of. When he opened them back up and saw a squirrel with little horns and bat wings hanging out on the dashboard scratching its belly, Ted froze, blinking a dozen times in the hopes the demonic fiend before him was a stress induced hallucination. Sadly for him, it was yet another topping on the sandwich of excrement the cosmos was making for him.

"Uli. What the shit is that?"

"My new familiar, his name is Blood Fucker! Made him this morning, Cute right?"

"No, it's not, it's terrifying." B.F. was not sure if to take that as a compliment or not.

"If anybody sees him you know how screwed you are? It's like you're waving a bag of drugs around Uli! You're gonna have me end up in jail too!"

"Relax! You said you needed more adventure, that your goalless life was chaining you to a hamster wheel of infinite despair and such."

"You said that."

"No I didn't, did I? Whatever, I always felt we were in the waiting room to something epic Ted! And it's here, in the trunk of all places!"

A canyon sized pothole made the car lift off enough to cause all present companies to pucker their butts in unison. They landed with a hefty bounce, dislodging the holiest of holy swords from its snug trunk seat, the grip of it dinging Uli hard in the head.

"Mother fucker!" Uli barked as she absorbed the blow. Ted coughed out a chuckle, for the fates finally directed their wrath on someone else.

His sample sized moment of joy was cut short after Ted realized the atomic pot hole they drove over was the one right outside Findar's Pizza Emporium.

Mark, Ted's teenage superior, stood crossed armed, doing his best bouncer power pose guarding the front door. The pimple farm apparently had been standing there for thirty minutes, savoring with despotic joy the haranguing he was about to unleash on the soon to be canned busser.

Did he have a past grievance with Ted? Perhaps bullied by him in his youth? Did Ted steal his girlfriend, pull down his pants, knock up his sister and murder his pet poodle Snuggles?

Nope, Mark was just a dick, that really got off pestering Ted. Why? Because he's a dick.

When Ted finally met his manager's gaze, his momentary smile went upside down instantly.

"Fuck," Ted muttered. Mark could read lips (cause he's a

dick like that) and displayed a grin for what was to come.

"How late are you?" Uli asked.

"Oh about forty nine minutes late. Wait here, if it goes how I think it will, I may need a ride home."

Ted got out of the car, put on his best lowly peasant smile and waved at Mark, to which the aforementioned dick did not return the pleasantry. Ted made it to the sidewalk before Mark brought up his arm signaling halt, "That's far enough Mr. Coalboar."

"Mark look, I know it's a little late but my car…"

"Mister Matras."

"Yeah sorry, Mr. Matras." Allowing himself some snark in the delivery, "My car, it broke down and I had to get a ride," Ted points behind him to Uli who only a second before managed to gently but promptly place her familiar in the backseat. She poked out the window, and gave a big enthusiastic wave, "Hey Marky! How ya doing buddy!?" Mark gave no return salute.

Mark proceeded to inform Ted of his many violations to the Findar way. As well as list out in great detail the infinite amount of strikes Ted had racked up throughout the years. Did Ted deserve to get fired? Yes. Did Mark have to be a dick about it? No.

Wile Ted received a winded verbal assault. Uli continued to admire the coffin sized sword hanging out the back of her car, wondering what stories transpired around it. Blood Fucker decided to match his masters curiosity and hopped on to the sword, running around its body trying to make heads or tails of the ancient thing. Perhaps discovering some ancient marking or rune to point out to the great and powerful Uli.

B.F. had a deep seeded need to please, he questioned

for a beat if that had always been a part of him, or was it programmed into him during his revivification. Such prolonged philosophical self exploration was a strain to him, plus the powers governing the laws of familiars made it so that any questioning of servitude should cause a level of discomfort.

The melding of these two concepts within Blood Fucker caused a terrible dizzy spell, culminating with him vomiting his acid bile right on the greatsword.

The chemical reaction was instant and vile, green smoke emanating from the disintegration of the rusted up garbage bracing to the particular section of the sword. Uli snagged B.F. up concerned both for the sword and her little critter, "Oh no, no, honey don't, not on the sword."

Mark eyed the smoke emanating from the station wagon, thinking to himself how much it made sense that Uli was into drugs, he then returned to the live autopsy of Ted's employment.

Once the smoke left the car, Uli checked the sword for any damage. The acid rather nicely ate away only the crud and rust, giving her a chance to see Dammerung's beauty. The spiraling galaxy-like patterns were a wonder to look at, its natural flowing grooves hypnotizing.

Uli's "Best day ever" just kept getting better and better. Without any common sense or hesitation, she went in for a touch of the recently exposed blade.

A cool, icy rush of energy traveled from her fingers to her core. She gasped, the air flowing into her feeling like she took a hit from a dozen menthol cigarettes. An azure glow emanated from the recently cleaned area, Uli had hoped it to be a magical weapon, but after feeling its presence expand in the car, she realized she was dealing with some pretty high quality, high powered stuff. Awesome? definitely, but a little bit scary too.

Ted had mentally checked out twenty seconds into his scolding, his attention on how red Mark's face was getting, and the accumulating saliva on the corners of the mean teen's lips, all while Ted pondered how much he would have actually gotten from his insurance had he kept up with the payments. His intrusive thought party was interrupted by the sound of wind chimes coming from Uli's station wagon.

"Hey, Coalboar! I'm talking to you man, look at me when I am firing you!" he did no such thing. Mark was about to load up another round of insults when the sound of metal tearing apart brought him to get a look for himself.

with an ear splitting rip, Dammerung popped out of the roof of Uli's station wagon, leaving in cartoonish detail its exit point. It arose to a vertical position with the grip and hilt pointing to the morning sky. Uli rolled out of the car, eyes transfixed on the slightly airborne blade. As for Mark and Ted, they stood in paralyzed awe.

"Oooooooooooooooooh you two, oh you two are so screwed! Magic?! Oh this is so great, Imma call the police, oh this is gold!" Mark was about to turn and make his way to the take out phone when the sword slowly moved from its hovering state down to floor level and made its way towards the restaurant.

"Uli! What you do?!"

"Nothing, Blood Fucker puked on it, I touched it and then…

Tadaaa!"

"Wait, you touched the puke?"

"No dummy, the sword!" Dammerung continued its slow and steady trek to the pasta barn. Ted politely got out of its way, but Mark stayed put having his fight or flight instinct glitch to full stasis.

"Oh shit!" Mark was transfixed, the floating relic inches away before he backed away tripping and falling.

Screaming like a wounded dog he dragged himself away from the sword, fearing it would get the urge to use him as his first kill of the day. He got himself up and ran inside locking the glass door entrance. The sword paid no mind and kept moving, the glass door crashed with little to no resistance.

Ted saw the scene straight out of a horror movie and couldn't help to feel a little glee from seeing the uppity teen look like a child about to get the belt from his father.

Uli took hold of Ted's arm and shook it.

"Um Teddy? What do we do!?"

"How the hell should I know, you're the one that knows about this stuff, turn it off!"

"Oh yeah, turn it off," Uli pondered.

"Do you know how?"

"Of course not! it's not like it has an on switch on it!"

"Did you check?"

This caused Uli pause, a switch? possible, but swords are not known to have them outside of the plastic light up ones kids can get at the bargain shops.

While Ted and Uli had their trouble shooting session, the sword had made its way to the host counter, tipping it over as it kept its straight trajectory to the kitchen. Nothing stopping its snail paced assault.

The duo made their way in and saw opening staff members hiding behind the newly installed salad bar. They followed Dammerung as it demolished its way to the kitchen down the fry cook aisle, Mark at the end of it balled up in the fetal position.

"Do something!" Ted begged, "I'm thinking! I'm thinking Okay!?" Uli said.

Ted was not known for being a man of action, but the only thing he could come up with was grabbing the sword from its grip hoping to slow it to a stop.

He grasped it and the sword up and stopped.

Mark, Ted and Uli exchanged glances, all three exhaling in relief. Mark hopped over the prep counter to the wall mounted phone.

"Mark come on, this is all just a misunderstanding, this ain't magic, it's a remote controlled prop Uli made for a short film."

The sword continued its lethargic path of havoc. Ted didn't let go, putting all his weight on the back of his heels, but the sword chugged along through the prep tables to the wall next to the emergency exit. Ted's knuckles cracked as the sword pressed against the drywall, he screamed and ripped his hands away before having them break from the intense pressure.

The sword broke through the wall and made it halfway through the back of house parking lot when it came to a dead stop, the melodic wind chime sounds coming from it turned off before it dropped from its levitating state, it panged and clattered to the black asphalt sounding like a giant tuning fork bouncing off an iron slab.

Uli helped Ted up, both peeking out the freshly punched hole in the wall. Ted's face was a tone whiter than milk, Uli was all smiles, both saying in unison, "Holy shit dude!" each with different emotional undertones to their delivery.

Distant police sirens screamed closer and closer. "You have to admire the response time of small town police, right Ted?" Mark said leaning on the wall next to the phone with a smirk more at home on a trickster god of old.

The cops were far enough for a plan to form, but close enough that any plan concocted would be a simple one.

"No, no, no, no, I didn't even do anything!"

"Don't matter Ted, magic happened in a public space," Uli pointed at Mark and the morning staff now peeking out over the mountain of shredded iceberg lettuce.

"I need to think!" Ted announced, one migraine away from an aneurysm.

"WE need to hide Ted!"

"Get the sword and let's get out of here!"

"Where?" asked Ted as he shoved open the emergency exit.

"To an expert!"

Mark would have given chase but decided against it, he was too busy using the wall to hide the fact that he had soiled his white acid wash jeans.

7

"Disturbance in the course"

The sun was shining upon the capital city of Vundirspire. White ivory and jade adorned the majority of the skyscrapers. The awe inspiring skyline was an eclectic mix of long preserved ruins and modern marvels of architecture.

At the center of this massive urban landscape is the Vundirspire capitol building, the beating heart of the Forlen dominion. Once a dread inducing fortress who's design and decor seemed inspired by the darkest of nightmares. Now several millennia later, has since been redesigned into a towering edifice fit for a jet setting elven forest queen, one hundred stories high, with a dozen botanical gardens, five copper sky domes, and guided tours every weekend from nine to three.

The only thing more impressive than the ode to beauty that is the Vundirspire capitol building, was the ballistic military might hiding just under its surface.

* * *

At the very top, standing at the edge of its rather lovely lookout balcony was a figure small in stature, but huge in presence. His ancient tunic flapped as his frail body stood steady against the powerful winds hammering the scenic view, this ancient affront to the laws of time was Volshtadt's right hand warlock and creator Kalammet.

The last remaining wizard of the grand council of Forlen was deep in thought, when he woke that morning, an unwanted air of warning hung around his mind making it difficult to concentrate.

The all seeing spell of Hilliden meditation is tricky, if done with sufficient magic and proper access to one the magical ley lines circulating within Thira, one is capable of having an actual god's eye view of anything happening on a global scale.

But with his rationed magic and the ley lines fading into oblivion. The most Kalammet could do was feel out what was happening in Thira.

His jet black eyes darting around as if dreaming in the deepest of rem sleep. The ley lines never liked him, Kalammet's magical attunement to the darker corners of spell work made him persona non grata to the magic super highway that is the ley line system.

The only thing he could discern was that something, somewhere flared up with magical energy, and then just turned off, as if never existing in the first place.

Threats to the rule of Volshtadt were few and far between, be it a small terrorist group that managed to hot wire a relic into exploding, or some green horn magic amateur accidentally activating a magical scroll turning a few dozen people to cows. All of these small potatoes which his clean up crews could silence at the drop of a hat.

But no little blip of arcane usage should be taken lightly, not when it's taken him and his creation Volshtadt dozens of lifetimes to erect the empire they now rule.

8

"President Volshtadt"

President Volshtadt gazed out the tremendous windows that surrounded his meeting room, he aimlessly looked at the kingdom he built, destroyed, and rebuilt until he got every little thing just perfect.

A gaggle of secretaries of defense, agriculture, transportation and sewage talked policy around the long conference table made of now antique iron wood. All of them discussed in varying levels of urgency last year's budgetary oversights, scandals, as well as how bad the tan was on Bob from accounting.

Volshtadt many times felt like they were speaking a different language. A dialect composed of numbers, groans, statistics and backhanded compliments.

He could, if the mood struck him, ask them all to get in a line, open the window and dive to their end. The idea made him smile, especially after the secretary of foreign relations asked in a bored tone if the good President "Understood the diplomatic implications of canceling the union summit with Voran Sammat?"

Eons of power and control could corrupt, or it could educate, And Volshtadt was cursed with a superior intellect designed to absorb information and mold to its most optimal usage. And lately it felt like his elegant execution of negotiations were more like entropy spells designed to make the rest of his life a living slog of an existence.

And since the only person who could have killed him was used as an equine landing cushion, the rest of his life was eternal, devoid of flavor and just down right dull.

The ping from the elevator snapped him out of his midday stupor.

"My King," echoed into the room as the warlock gave a reverential bow, Kalammet never enjoyed calling his creation anything else than King or My Lord. Mr. President is fine for the modern peons, but in his own twisted sense of ego, his living weapon of mass destruction will always be dubbed King.

The various department heads looked at the dark wizard's arrival with mild contempt and fear.

Being one of the last living practitioners of magic, and the last living survivor of Volshtadt's original era, gave him an aura of mystery and power that made him scary enough not to mess with, yet it separated him from their reality enough to complain about him around the water cooler.

Volshtadt greeted his right hand with a limp, "Hello wizard."

"My King, I come to you in regards too..." Kalammet halted his report, they still had an audience, he gave them his best evil glare to which the office grunts promptly got the hell out of there.

Everyone except for the newly appointed Secretary of Rural Relations Herfin Jenkins, the mild mannered monument to khaki sat confused, this was as you lot like to say "His first rodeo," and probably his last.

"We've pushed the budget meetings back three times already, we do it one more time and who knows how the unions will react," Jenkins said, with a level of sincerity alien to 98.5% of the humans that dare dub themselves "servants of the people."

Volshtadt locked eyes with the man and smiled, the grin devoid of all warmth but a polite one nonetheless, Jenkins returned the gesture.

"You're new here right? Jenkins is it?" asked Volshtadt in a friendly tone.

"Yes sir, It's been three weeks."

"Have the veteran staffers been welcoming to you?"

"Oh yes, thank you sir. Very! And very helpful in filling me in on the ins and outs of it all."

"It seems they didn't fill you in on everything."

"Excuse me sir?"

"Do you know how gravity magic works Herfin?"

If the good Herfin Jenkins was confused at first, now he was as lost as a child in a mega mall.

"Sir? I don't know what that has to do…"

"Back in the day, most folk with any talent would find out which attunement they had in the great variety of magics. Mine was a very rare one, gravity magic."

Volshtadt casually lifted his right hand and cracked his index knuckle, the pop was loud and crisp, Jenkins raised an eyebrow to the awkward air now prevalent in the office, he was about to say something when an unseen force pressed him into his chair.

"Doesn't sound as flashy as the elemental or manifesting types of spell work, but it fits my personality just fine."

Volshtadt popped his middle finger, summoning several pounds of force on Jenkins' head, his spine audibly compressing, lighting up his nerve endings in sudden and excruciating pain.

Kalammet watched queerly to the subtle signs of pleasure manifesting on his king's face. For many a century he never saw any inkling of blood lust in his dark champion, and now, today of all days he got to see a glimpse to the past murderous passion Volshtadt was known for.

"When my right hand gives you the look, you get out, I'm surprised they didn't give you the heads up, sadly some lessons are learned too late in life right?"

Volshtadt had locked and loaded his ring finger for a real doozy of a pop.

"My King. A good secretary of rural relations has proven a difficult position to fill as of late, perhaps his warning could be of the less lethal variety?"

Volshtadt lazily looked up to Kalammet, exhaling from his nostrils loud enough to announce his disappointment, "Very well, so sorry Jenkins, we'll get back to the budget tomorrow," he popped his pinkie finger releasing the G-force applied to his now wet pantsed Secretary of rural relations.

Jenkins gasped for air, letting out a winded "Yes sir, see you tomorrow sir," he proceeded to drag himself out of the office.

Volshtadt raised from his seat and lit up a smoke, "To what do I owe you saving me from yet another budget meeting?"

"A spike of Eitherkreiss near the capitol my King."

"Probably another antique shop owner rubbing a lamp the

wrong way?"

"Its signature was odd, bit older than the ones we've dealt with, something about it gave me an ill sensation at the pit of my stomach."

Volshtadt snorted out smoke in amusement "The great and powerful Kalammet, has a hunch? You've…we've lived far too long, you're just getting too paranoid in your old age, send some of your errand boys to get rid of the problem and be done with it."

"Two units are in the general area, but I lost contact with them yesterday."

"You think this is related," asked Volshtadt.

"Coincidences should never be taken lightly."

Volshtadt stared at his advisor while he took a long final drag to his smoke. He turned and exhaled the gray cloud, it undulated to a forgotten corner of office space. One where his ancient war ravaged armor was on display.

Calling magic by its ancient name of Eitherkreiss gave him a pang of melancholy, to a simpler time, before budget meetings, fake elections and union strikes.

To a fun time, of blood and conquest.

"My King? Perhaps we should."

"Was it worth it my wizard?" Volshtadt interrupted.

"What was?"

Volshtadt waved to the office, the city skyline, the well oiled machine of conformity they had so painstakingly built.

"Causality always favored the light, in this error, in this botched equation, we found freedom, freedom from prophecy, from destiny, and only your hand made it so," Kalammet proclaimed with a preacher's conviction. Volshtadt rubbed his eyes, the old way of speaking of his right hand had been sanding down his patience as of late.

"I fear that something conspires to break our grip, best not to…"

"I'm tired Kalammet. I must rest."

"Very good, But?" asked the wizard, with a tone of worry.

"Leave it be, if the drakenstatz don't come back online, just tell the local authorities to look into a bomb threat or something of its kind"

"But my King…"

"LEAVE IT BE."

Kalammet averted his eyes as he bowed in compliance.

Volshtadt snuffed out his smoke on the conference table and hopped over the puddle of piss Jenkins left behind.

"You have too much free time wizard, take up a hobby or two, I've been told the older cattle enjoy jogging in malls."

A waiting elevator took Volshtadt away, leaving his high advisor alone in the empty conference room.

Wise, ruthless and ever vigilant was his king, but the many years of peace through dulling the masses had made Volshtadt uninterested and careless. The fact that he saw the Voidlord prepared to pancake an employee on a whim, made the coincidences add up a bit too quickly for his liking.

And too many coincidences in a row add up to not being a coincidence at all. Fate was a word he had not manifested in his mind for centuries, but it felt like that ugly little word wanted to make a comeback.

And words like that don't have a place in the world they made, he'll make sure of it.

9

"Scatter Lands"

In life you only really get four or five people that understand you. Either through mutual interest, a connecting traumatic pain, or just the fact they share your sick sense of humor. Lucky for Uli she had Ted, and crazy Aunt Ogun.

If black sheep is your term of choice, you could say her wool was midnight black covered in prehistoric oil. Aunt Ogun had no job, no kids and no contact with the outside world, and Uli loved the ever loving shit out of her. Being one of the few true historians of the ancient extinct nations, Uli could get an endless stream of stories and historical happenings from a world that she felt more like home than her very own slice of rural living.

Ogun is one of the few outlaw spellslingers still around. She was the first to see Uli's affinity for the dead-er branches of the arcane.

Magic magnifies itself with the bearer's interests and creativity. During the golden age of sorcery, most were given this godspark, the ability to create and manifest thought the means of magic, and back in the day if you had enough of it, you could make some wild stuff pop into reality and call yourself a witch, wizard or warlock. Today that godspark is so diluted, only a few can tap into its ever dwindling presence, opting for less ostentatious practices, such as the arts, marketing and dare I say the taboo practice of a communications degree.

Auntie Ogun kept her niece's training in the old ways secretive. Ancient texts and exercises practiced on sleepovers, or when the folks were at book club meetings where reading was optional, and snorkeling in box wine was obligated.

When Uli would get a little self conscious about learning how to bring dead things back to life, Ogun would give some wise words like "No such thing as evil magic, it's what the person does with it," a somewhat flimsy argument, but children aren't known for investigating empirical evidence.

* * *

Now wanted from the law, gods knows what the police are probably telling Uli's parents about her at that very moment, but she had bigger things to focus on, they had to lay low and get some answers, and if anybody had any idea on what to do with a magically boosted big ass sword, as well as being a bit hard to find, that would be her favorite relative of all time.

Getting to Ogun's was a pain in the toosh. Deep in the Scatter Lands, where housing was scarce and the tree lines thick. Unkempt serpentine roads made it a slow going slog, perfect for hashing out any and all grievances one could have with their best friend, and Ted and Uli were taking said opportunity.

"Maybe you can apologize and like do extra hours or something," Uli suggested as she focused on not love tapping every tree on the way to Ogun's.

"It doesn't work that way Uli, property was damaged, and Mark thought we were gonna kill him."

"Yeah, but we didn't do anything, it was the sword, we just blame it all on the sword."

"And who brought it there? who turned it on? Who has their fingerprints on it, us! *Thindren fucking Crytrunk*, how did I manage to get fired and become a criminal on the same day?!"

"Also broken up with," Uli added.

Ted bit into his arm and screamed as hard as he could.

"There you go big guy, just like Dr. Thorn on the morning show said, scream out, peace in, scream out, peace in."

"I was happy Uli!" Blood Fucker popped out of Uli's satchel, not liking one bit the way Ted was talking to his master, one more outburst like that and he conspired to rid the miserable human of the two nuts he is hiding in his undies.

"No you weren't."

"I had a great job!"

"You hated it."

"A good woman."

"She said at parties she dated you out of pity."

"A home and a good car!"

"You rented a motor home, and your car had exhaust fumes in the cabin."

"But it was my life Uli! It was a mess, but a functional one, and that thing in the back and YOU ruined it all!"

"Well yeah, but It's a sign big guy!" that last comment

required another scream into Ted's arm.

"I don't want signs or magic or or or adventure Uli, I just want my life back, my nice, quiet, life."

"It wasn't living Ted, it was just existing, and you, I and everyone deserve a bit more than that, you see that sword as a curse, but maybe it was just the thing to give you what you deserve my dude, a GOOD life!" Uli was about to rev up another assault of positive thinking but held back, Ted's nose was running and his eyes got a darker tone of red with every tear he was holding back.

"Look, let Ogun check the thing out, if she says it's not worth our trouble that'll be the end of it. I'll call my dad and have him meet up with us at your place, we'll explain how it totaled your car and Pop can say that we were on our way to hand it over to the cops but I had to take you to work. He gave the police station free cable so they kind of owe him, okay?"

Ted's bullshit detector flashed red, but the idea of getting rid of the thing that had cursed his life sounded like a good deal. He wiped off his snot and rubbed his eyes raw.

"Fine, as long as we get rid of it."

"But who knows! Maybe that thing back there is OUR destiny calling!"

"No it isn't..."

"Our quest for justice and glory!"

"Please stop."

"Our ultimate truth! And stuff."

"Please stop talking."

"Come on Ted, you're not some farm dud waiting your turn down the slaughter house slide. You're Ted Coalboar! descendant of the berserker tribes of Guantilthok! Those dudes were fearless!"

"Turns out we are only 5% Gauntik."

"Oh. Bummer, still, that's like five percent more than me, so, there you go."

The tunnel of arching trees broke open to a clearing, a small barn without animals, couple of busted up cars missing all their tires and a weathered trailer home decorated the run down but quaint witch hideout.

"I forgot how much your aunt's place looks like a serial killers home base."

"Awesome right? But no, sure it's hidden, but terrible for hiding bodies, deserts are better, plenty of open space and less animals large enough to dig them up to later be found by hikers."Any other person would have recoiled at Uli's interests, but Ted knew she couldn't help it, she always talks about death when she's excited. And even though his life has gone to shit, and in no small part thanks to Uli, he did love seeing that milk face with too much eye shadow grin like an excited idiot.

10

"Auntie Ogun"

Uli slowed the car to a full stop before crossing the perimeter fence made of shipping pallets.

"When's the last time you saw her?" Ted said.

They rolled in close enough to see every window on the trailer home shattered.

They parked away from the home, Ted afraid to peek outside of the imagined safety of the car.

"What do we do, call the cops?" asked Ted.

"No, not yet, plus wanted criminals and all," Uli said while opening her car door. Ted reached over and closed it right back.

"Oh no you don't, you want our footprints at two crime scenes in the same day?"

"Cool your paranoid jets, I just want to see if Aunt Ogun is still there or not."

"But what if she's dea…" Ted shut the hell up. Uli frowned at where Ted's question was going.

She stepped out and quietly made her way towards the trashed home, she looked back to Ted waving her hand aggressively to get his freckled ass out there.

Though not one hundred percent yellow, Ted does need from time to time a moment to ponder and deliberate if he has enough bravery stored up toward the mission at hand. Before he had a chance to mentally weigh out the pros and cons, Uli let out a "tired of your bullshit" laced sigh.

"Fine, guard the car or whatever," she whispered disappointedly as she made her way to the trailer door, she unsheathed her knockoff ceremonial dagger from her bag, gently as to not disturb Blood Fucker from his bag time siesta.

"Holy shit," Ted said quietly at the badassery of his friend.

But Uli always made sure to carry protection, it's a scary world out there, for girls and magic users alike.

Ted saw Uli tiptoe through the open front door.

He had a healthy amount of jealousy to Uli's natural gumption. Deep down in some lost corner of Ted's guts was something that made him, despite many a dicey situation, stay close to Uli, call it fear for Uli's safety, or fear for his, but it never felt right leaving Uli alone.

Plus, she took the car keys, and if some nipple eating serial killer was gonna make Uli his dinner, it was gonna be super hard to get the keys once that whole scenario plays out.

Ted rolled down the window and quietly yelled "Hey!" Uli stuck her head out the door, shushing him.

He mouthed out "Wait up" and got out of the car. In that moment he got back whatever points he lost in Uli's friendship book. He caught up and crossed the threshold into the dark and spooky trailer home.

Uli had a grizzled detective scowl as she scanned the place.

But she was one bump in the dark away from pooping her bat print panties.

The few sunbeams strong enough to make it through the shredded curtains showed the home ransacked, couches trashed and tables flipped over. "Shit," Ted said quietly to himself.

Aunt Ogun's abode usually looked this way, always trying out spells and such, some just got out of hand, the obliterated windows were the only new addition to the standard mess.

Ted's placed chairs upright in silent slow motion as they traversed the chaos of the living room.

"Nobody's here," whispered Ted.

A sour, rotted stench crept up both their noses the closer they got to the kitchen. Uli's necromantic sensibilities had her more used to the smell of the recently deceased.

Uli ran in, visions of her favorite relative splayed out on the floor in a pool of her own blood, dead, alone, left there to rot. Her stomach went to knots, in her mind a voice telling her to brace herself, this was going to probably suck, one of the two people she genuinely likes could be gone forever now.

She saw a form under the kitchen table. She tilted her head enough to get a better peek.

"Oh damn."

"What? She's dead isn't she, fuck!" Ted said pacing around in a panic.

She waved him over to get a gander. Covering his nose Ted peeked under the table for half a second.

"What the actual hell dude!" he said as he twisted away from what looked like two dead men in suits splayed out on the checkered linoleum floor.

"Neither of them Aunt Ogun."

"You sure?"

"You would never catch her wearing black, she doesn't have huge broad shoulders, and um, that."

"What?"

Uli knelt next to the bodies and moved the head of one of them enough to get a good look at the face, the whole action was done so casually that it reminded Ted of those crime scene procedural shows Uli would force him to watch.

"They're covered in scales," Uli said, impressed.

Ted brought his shirt over his nose, "Ya think it's contagious?" Uli tapped the neck of one of the downed creatures, marble hard and coarse, feeling more stone-like in texture than the refined armored plating she was expecting.

"It's dragon scale," A surprise voice interrupted.

Ted and Uli jumped in random directions raising their hands in defense at whatever the unseen attacker had ready for them.

Uli's face lit up with actual color."Auntie Ogun! You're alive!"

"Of course I am baby, I'm insulted you thought my ancient ass was in trouble." There she stood with her salt and peppered mess of hair that made her stand out at every family get together, face wrinkled but still noting her natural sun dried beauty, her indoor robe tattered, showing out from it her plaid shirt and ripped jeans.

"What are those things?" Ted asked.

"Dragonsacks!" exclaimed Ogun. "At least that's what we've been calling these things. Makes ya think about dragon nuts don't it? All dangling and such? But the name just stuck, some alchemist's came up with these bastards a while back by grafting dragon scales on humans."

Ogun, unfazed, promptly slid around her busted up kitchen to make some tea for everyone.

"Word on the grapevine is that these critters here have been fetching up magic users left and right."

"Isn't that a, um, like a cop thing? Picking up wizards and stuff?" Ted asked.

"Right you are Tiny," she pointed with a dirty spoon to the dragonsack twins. "But these little critters have been popping up more often than the fuzz."

"Wouldn't the police have noticed this stuff?"

"Why? They don't know these missing folk are magically inclined, all they see is random disappearances, and even if they had a suspicion of these guys and gals doing magic, I wouldn't be surprised if they didn't mind that these monsters are saving them the hassle of processing perps."

With a fire spark from her finger she boiled the water instantly in the kettle, expertly serving them some of her patented mug wort tea (horrible name, lovely taste).

"So how the hell did you manage to take them on auntie?" Ogun's eyes sparked up wide as she smiled a villain's grin,"With this."

Ogun opened the dishwasher and pulled out a piece of black stone, sharp and shaped like a prison shiv.

"Argonite, once I saw the scales on the bastards I knew magic wasn't gonna work on them, This sharp little bugger works like a charm."

"So you're saying these guys are actual dragons?" Ted asked, confused. "I thought they were bigger and had wings."

The last lot of dragons were put down thousands of years ago, people were over breeding them, making them smaller and smaller till they were the size of a pocket dog, the species couldn't be further artificially evolved, and what was left of them was too mutated and inbred that they just died off.

"Dragons could appear as humans, but these things are different, when a dragon molts into a human, they lose their scales, but not these boys, they are fully decked in them, I've been hiding in the basement, in case anybody came looking, but you're the first two that have come around in days."

Ogun's ears twitched to the faint sound of wind chimes, "But that's not why you came over today, is it?"

11

"Welcome to the light show"

Ted dragged the refrigerator sized sword to Ogun's basement workshop. The dimly lit space would make any sorcerer or medieval fair enthusiast feel right at home. Boiling flasks of multicolored liquids, shelves of random bones and herbs, the real deal.

He placed the sword on top of an already cluttered picnic table that served as the forest witch's work table.

"Where did this little beauty come from?" asked Ogun.

"Space, landed on my car."

"Sometimes I think you're cursed Teddy boy."

"Sometimes I think you're right."

"Out of the sky huh? That's some ancient foretold omen shit right there."

"That's what I said! But Ted wouldn't believe me," Uli said, proud she had at least the same amount of intuition as a seasoned veteran.

"But, if it was one of them ANCIENT OMENS FORETOLD BY THE GODS OF FATE! I think someone would have mentioned something in the back channels about an eighty percent chance of sword showers with mild precipitation."

"But it hit Ted's car, maybe it was meant for him."

"One way to find out, we just have to jog the poor thing's memory."

"You're gonna what now?" Ted scoffed. Uli ran in place squealing sporting a wide tooth grin. They were gonna get a show!

Ogun gathered powders and potions from all around the mold invaded basement, mixed and matched them into the cutest tiny cauldron in the far end of the basement.

"Every object has a story to it, Every scratch, every dent leaves a notch on the timeline, an enchanted recording." The trailer home dwelling conjurer poured a pint's worth of the concoction over the sword, the blade levitated horizontally off the table by a few inches as Ogun basted it honey baked ham style with the potion. The crusted up space mildew cracked off of its every edge and corner. Revealing its long hidden otherworldly beauty.

Uli's eyes and mouth were wide in geeky wonder. Though she diligently practiced at home and in forgotten places around town, her own ability could never touch the prowess of Auntie Ogun.

The hair on the back of every neck present stood up, throw in a dose of Uli's own adrenaline, and moments like these serve as a reminder to her why she loves the giant middle finger to reality that is magic. The little girl in her smiled from ear to ear and said to herself in silent reverence.

"Magic is the shit."

"WELCOME TO THE LIGHT SHOW"

Ted was more terrified than caught up in arcane whimsy. He never had anything against magic or the few secret practitioners of it, live and let live and all that jazz, but if pointy space trash was going to say something like "Ted has to go on a quest or else humanity is doomed and shit," he was going to throw up and defecate himself to death, and he was fine with that if it meant avoiding just everything his life has become as of late.

The lights dimmed as holographic images danced and twirled around the sword like a fairy powered carousel. Faces and places from a bygone time spurred to life. Ogun saw it all with a mild amusement, it's not that she's jaded, she just needs to play the part of world weary master.

"You wanna hit the play button?" she offered Uli, as she ran a finger over the projections accelerating the images like a sci fi hologram player. Uli nodded yes so violently she got minor whiplash. Ogun placed Uli's hand on the blade "Okay sweety, showtime!" Uli slid her finger off the sword triggering the sights and sounds to play out at its appropriate speed.

Enter a humongous blacksmith swinging a hammer heavier than a dead star, each gravity crunching hit blew out sparks the size of hot dog wieners, yes, I said hot dog wieners.

Bolts of lightning struck the blacksmith with every strike upon the white hot anvil.

The smith fell to the floor dead from the effort of molding such condensed magic. His last breath barely exhaled when another smith would pick up the hammer and continue the labor. Like a barbarian war god mid climax, the buck naked blacksmith yelled his life out with every effort.

A small army of long cloaked wizards etched and sharpened the sword. All gaunt as corpses on the verge of turning into dust, but nothing deterred their duty of honing the blade to perfection.

Ogun and company watched the multicolored galaxies floating within the sword swirl in an infinite spiral through the space confined in the blade. This was obviously not the birth of some standard steel poker for a nobody, this was special. A ritual performed a handful of times, due to the toll it took on reality itself.

A living dimension, another world with even more infinite worlds within, forged into a weapon.

A being made of blazing light lifted the finished sword, he went to a fighting stance performing slash after elegant slash, A hurricane's roar came with every simulated attack.

"Holy poo poo dude." Ted was of Barbarian blood (five percent but still,) even with his dumb genetically boosted ox strength he couldn't even fathom moving that much metal so easily.

Ogun fingered the hologram ahead in time to a chiseled face with a smile that could rival the sun's radiance.

Only prince Aiden had that presence, the chosen one in his armor ready for the battle ahead, sword in hand, glowing like a neon saint, the data hit Ogun like a wrecking ball.

She gasped, covered her mouth, losing all ability to think, all she could whisper out was the prophecy.

"From hand of chosen man, shall the Dammerung slay the dark lord's command! "

"What?" Ted asked.

"Shut up Ted!" Uli answered.

"WELCOME TO THE LIGHT SHOW"

It was the battle at Alzahar crater.

The unfortunate holographic documentary proceeded to show what transpired on that horrid night. That included the whole horse slipping on dookie, and said horse smashing the hero's life out of him.

Ogun and Ted looked away at how a horse made Aiden's spine collapse into itself. Oh but not Uli, always a sucker for a good gory matinee, and so far this was a masterpiece.

The dark armored menace known as Volshtadt approached the fallen hero, his eyes set on the Dammerung sword.

"Is that who I think it is?" asked Uli.

They witnessed Volshtadt attempt to destroy the sword. Ogun sped through the many attempts as it was getting old quick. What caught Ogun's eyes was how it hurt the dark messiah to brandish the blade. The hiss of scalding skin erupted from his hands, pain drenched screams poured out of him with every second he held on to it.

His desperation obvious, he gripped it one last painful time and launched into outer space.

"So that's where it went," Ogun said.

"What went where?" Ted asked.

They turned back to see more snippets on Dammerung's cosmic adventure, gelatinous mobs of aliens crash into each other in gloppy combat as Dammerung ominously towered over them.

"That…is worth looking into later," Ogun forwarded one more time. She let it play out in real time seconds before it blew up Ted's car. Ogun couldn't help but laugh at Ted's impressively sustained bad luck.

Ted in the remembrance screamed in such a manner that it sounded more like a child getting stung by a whole beehive.

"A big chunk of metal from space blew up my car, I'm allowed to scream."

"Yeah," said Ogun, "Just not like that."

"Men are allowed to scream and cry now Ogun!" remarked Ted with a whimper stuck in his throat (gender equality was progressing in Thira, but it was more baby steps than elephant strides).

"Calm down big boy, I'm only screwing with ya."

"Ahem!" Uli said, coughing it out as if to cut the comedy skit escalating before her.

"Sorry, you guys still don't recognize it?"

Ted and Uli stared blankly at Ogun. *"Elema's* ghost, what are they teaching you kids in school?"

Both brains were turned on, but regardless, file not found.

"It's the sword, you know THE sword, the holiest of holy, the only thing created that could kill the then Dark Lord Volshtadt."

Uli's brain swan dived into her stomach, then exploded back into her skull for her to blurt out, "It can kill the president?!"

"Bingo to the short young lady in the front."

Ogun filled them in on the fact that everything they knew about the history of Thira was a well crafted, perfectly edited pile of bullshit, created to build the lie that Volshtadt was a unifier, only bits and pieces of the true history of the world existed, and if the higher ups ever found out you had an old book or two, your life was a that moment null and forfeit.

After taking all that info about a chosen one, evil kings and magic swords galore, Uli, bug eyed and giddy points at her best bud, "Ooh! Ooh! a chosen one! Chosen one!"

"Gods no," Ogun laughed "Can you even imagine?"

"Rude." Ted snarled.

"What? Like you wanted the job?" snarked Ogun.

"Granted, but the fact that you made it sound so ludicrous still hurt."

"I'm so sorry fair maiden," Ogun joked as she did a half assed bow.

"That is sexist and condescending."

"You're right, I'm sorry dumb ass, that better?"

"I know you're being dickish, but yes, that was better."

"So am I a chosen one?" Uli excited at the possibilities."It glowed when I touched it and stuff."

"Sorry baby. Dammerung is a living dimension made of light magic, it uses its wielder as an anchor to summon its power in this plane of reality, it was made for one man and one man alone, Aiden Pollthic, and as you just witnessed, he's not with us anymore, the fact it reacted to you is just the magic in ya, you got the goods, but it's not the flavor the sword vibes with the most."

Ogun sipped her tea, organizing her thoughts on what to do next, fate and destiny left the world a long time ago, leaving Thira in a perpetual state of "What now?" if this was fated or just happenstance, it was something to not only take note of, but to exploit.

"On your way here, did anyone see you with it?"

"Cops were coming our way, but we left before they got there."

Ted had filled his quota of adventure and bad luck for the day, or possibly the year. But the snowball of shit he felt gathering speed before him caused every hole in his body to pucker up for impact.

Though genuinely relieved about not being the main character of whatever hell the other two were concocting, Teddy couldn't help but feel a bit insulted, when the two of the most important people in your life would probably feel safer if the chosen one was a one legged raccoon.

"So you're sure I'm not the chosen one?" asked Uli.

"Would you quit it with the whole chosen thing. There are no chosen ones anymore okay? Haven't been for a good long while. Volshtadt and his goons made good on that. Every oracle, soothsayer and nut job on the planet that even farted out a word about visions were smeared out of existence. Even without prophecy, after Prince Aiden bit the dust, the whole chosen one business closed due to fate being proved wrong."

"So what now? We have two rotting corpses with dragon scales, a holy sword with no owner. Is all this just dead on arrival?" Uli said.

"Who knows? Sure magic works in mysterious ways, but the sword at this point is just an old hunk of metal better used as garden decor at a roadside museum, no chosen one, no *"From hand of chosen man, shall the Dammerung slay the dark lord's command."*

"Sounds good to me," Ted exhaled in relief.

"Of course it does, to you," Uli said, letting her cadence announce her disdain for Ted's chicken shittery.

"Look, we have to address each problem at a time. Those things up stairs tried to kill me or take me," Uli said.

Ted and Uli nodded along, Uli because she wanted answers, Ted because his many years in mindless staff meetings had taught him to nod and let the big brains figure the thing out, as to finish the damn meeting early and go home.

"They came for me, even before you two brought the sword."

"Still to treat everything that happened as coincidence wouldn't be smart," Uli said, impressing her aunt with her worldly and weathered words.

"I hate it when you sound smart," Ted said.

"So" Uli turned to look at her aunt "What are WE going to do?"

Lucky for them, Blood Fucker was about to help out with that answer.

12

"Blood Fucker is bored"

Uli introduced her familiar to Ogun, and her aunt couldn't be prouder of her aspiring mage. Uli put him down and let him have some post nap play time. Ogun, Ted and Uli went back upstairs for refills and brainstorming. Blood Fucker was left to putter around the basement, squirrels need their cardio after all, and using an underground laboratory as your own personal obstacle course is an opportunity no recently reanimated woodland creature should squander.

The squirrel version of "The floor is lava" (which in his culture was known as "bear poop puddle jump.") was his game of choice for the moment, mostly due to the fact that it was one of the few games he could play by himself, the humans were busy and the only other animals in the basement were the ones in pickling jars, and that family of cockroaches under the bookshelf that were a bit racist.

He hopped, sprang and dashed over the floors with the grace and speed of a cocaine fueled ninja. His vestigial wings flapped around, serving far less as tools of flight and more as indicators of the fun he was having.

He reached the main picnic/operating table and had planned to slide along the flat side of Dammerung's blade and end the run with a front flip off it, followed by a couple of casual, classy tumbles.

The set up was sound, and B.F. was more than capable of the acrobatic feat at hand. The factor he did not take into consideration was what would happen when he came into contact again with a magically charged sword. A self-sentient familiar he was, but a marvel in the memory department was not his strong suit.

He leaped onto the sword, the undulating, vibrating song of the now active sword came alive when it touched his poofy little paws.

The table rattled (as did Blood Fucker's teeth,) from the smacking of the sword's cross guard. it hovered over the table with Blood Fucker riding like it was the worlds most wicked looking skateboard.

With a whoosh and a crash it bursted up into the kitchen, B.F. took first contact with the old stuccoed basement roof, crushing him like a soda can in a fur cozy.

Ted, Uli and Ogun let out a high pitched yelp.

"It's doing it again! Is it supposed to do that?!" asked Ted.

"Your guess is as good as mine," Ogun said, "This is my first time dealing with history altering magical swords."

The fevered hum and wind chime harmonics of the blade rang in everyone's ears, it decided then to do a repeat of his Pasta Barn rampage and destroyed its way out of Ogun's home.

A pause accentuated the pitter patter of trash falling from the hole left from lift off. "Perfect, it's gone," Ted said, exhaling a relieved breath. "We can just put all this behind us, thank gods."

B.F. broken and beaten hopped off the blade, he tried to stick the landing but managed only a very entertaining face plant.

"Yeah it did that last time too, then it just dropped dead," Uli said.

As if by command Dammerung petered out, landing on the bed of dead leaves adorning Ogun's front yard.

"You guys heard it right?" Uli said, "How can a sword cry out like that?"

"It's looking for his buddy, his partner."

"But he's like super dead now. And who knows where his old bones even are?"

"He was buried in a secret location," Ogun said.

"Yeah but why hide it?" Uli asked.

"It could be a thousand reasons or just one, the people could have used his dead body as a symbol, or made a monument so we would never forget him. But long story short, they just didn't want people fucking with it. There was a lot of speculation on what happened to Aiden's body, some say it was burned, some say it was chopped up, his parts scattered across the planet. Others just said Volshtadt ate him up and absorbed his powers. I mean sure, "Evil King" and such, But despite all the shit he did, he never really struck me as a fan of cannibalism."

"So, what? Help the doggy brained sword find the final resting place of its master?" Uli pouted. It sounded like a good enough adventure, but escort missions are the bottom of the barrel when it came to grand questing. "Complete the burial" didn't have a cool ring to it either.

Ogun had developed a headache, she always said headaches are good for thinking, a peaceful happy mind doesn't look for answers, it's a grumpy pissed off one that has the power to get shit done and get on with it.

They have the one thing that can kill the immortal ruler, but every sword has its mate, and this one's owner has been long dead. Even if they found Aiden and let the sword rest with his designated chosen one, what good would that do?

Ogun distractedly looked at Blood Fucker had made his way back and was chowing down on the head of the leader cockroach from downstairs, thus ending its bigoted reign of terror.

An epiphany birthed to life right before her.

"It's right there!" Ogun pointing at Uli's decayed familiar. "Right there, staring at our fucking faces."

Ted and Uli followed Ogun's line of sight to Blood Fucker. They now had questions, Even B.F. was perplexed.

"What? Is the squirrel the chosen one now? We're screwed," Ted scoffed.

"Gods, if you just could have been good looking, But the higher powers didn't even bless you with that did they?" Ogun said.

"You're not a nice lady," Ted said, sipping a beer he stole from the fridge, he lost his job, maybe a future in alcoholism was his true calling.

Ogun focused on Uli "Hun, it's you."

"But I thought I wasn't THE chosen one," Uli said.

"Well you're not."

"I, I'm still lost."

"You have magic don't you?"

"I do yeah."

"And what type is it?"

Uli looked at her putrid but cute pet, her single brain cell decided to tap in now. "Oh shit! But, but, but I am an apprentice Necromancer, I've never brought something bigger than Blood Fucker."

"True, your magic isn't strong enough to bring back a human, let alone a chosen one, we need one more Necromancer, we need Oman."

Ogun waddled herself to the living room.

She slipped a big strapped pouch over her shoulder and limped around collecting trinkets and survival gear stuffing them into a big self made bag.

"The prophecy!" Said Ogun with a manic laugh, "The fucking prophecy, all the translations and interpretations, nobody figured it out," Ted heard the glee in Ogun's speech and felt a cold sweat run from his back to his butt cheeks. Things are getting set in motion, and that was one of about two hundred anxiety triggers Ted had on the ready.

"From hand of chosen man, shall the Dammerung slay the dark lord's command! Didn't say anything about Aiden having to be alive and kicking," she continued to sing the prophecy."No wonder they burned all the Necromancers with all their books , they didn't want anybody getting ideas!" Ogun was achieving a high from multiple dots connecting at once.

She opened a dusty old chest and pulled out a copper cylinder covered in primitive hieroglyphics. She blew the dust off it and handed it to Uli.

"What's this?"

"A one time resurrection spell made for the master Necromancer Oman Zurr! You get him up and going and he can be your second in the ritual."

"Who's that?"

"One of the first Necromancers. Got his resurrection scroll at a less than legal flea market a few years back. When I realized what it was, I got worried someone would bring the old coot back, he was the scab of Thira way before our President was."

"Where is he?"

"The markings on the container gave directions to his tomb, figured out it's under the Luminous Lakes Mall a few towns over, bit run down, great corn dogs though."

"You just said the guy is bad news, what if he starts a war or joins Volshtadt?" Ted asked, there was logic to his proposal, but Ted knew he's not that logical or lucky ever.

"We'll just bring his head back, no body, no problem I say," Ogun looked at Uli, "What do you say honey girl? Wanna bring back an ancient Necromancer's head to life to teach you the ways of the undead, revive Prince Aiden and rid the world of the Evil King once and for all?"

Uli pumped her fists in the sky and with no hesitation belted out "YEEEEEEEEEAAAAAAAH!!!!!" Ogun followed suit and did the same till looking like two ancient humans doing a very crude ritualistic dance.

"Hell no! we brought the sword to your aunt, found out what it is and that's fine, but I draw the line on resurrections followed up by killing the President!"

"Technically he's kind of a god king, so deicide would be a more appropriate term..." Ogun couldn't help but interject.

"Oh I'm sorry, deicide! So um yeah, no, big nope, I'm done here, you gals got this," Ted gave them both a thumbs up and made his way to the front door, "You two have fun on your two person death march."

"TED!" Uli said, locking eyes with him. She raised her right hand in front of her, pointing her index and middle finger straight at Ted's forehead.

"No, please don't," Ted cowered away from the tiny young lady. Uli was stone faced, as much as she loves (as a friend) her freckled giant, she had to pull this big gun out of mental storage. She needs him for this, and she needs him to move now before the momentum is lost.

"You give me no choice, I'm cashing in the DEBT OF OZEN MALOIQUE!"

If it was raining, a couple of thunder strikes would have accented the ominous and hard to pronounce words.

"Uh, What's an Ozen Maloique?" Asked Ogun, Before Uli could vocalize a single syllable, Ted screamed in a panicked horror more at home on a direct to V.H.S. horror flick.

"Don't you dare tell her what Ozen Maloique is!"

"Shit on a stick! Now I really wanna know!"

"By the laws of friendship, I command you to fulfill your duty!" Uli said.

"No! Why!? Come on! You had to use it on this?"

"We are on the verge of something serious, felt like the right place to use it."

Ted had no choice, it was either submit to the ancient and binding pact of Ozen Maloique, or lose the only person that's given a single fuck about him.

Ogun and B.F. stood in silence by the drama charged pressure these two were throwing out. It was both awkward and super fun to watch.

Ted looked at her through his bushy eyebrows, doing his best and most honest pissed off face. He broke the stare and went to the fridge, pulled out two more beers, and chugged them one after the other. He ended his theatrics with a Ted sized three beer boosted burp.

"Fine," Ted said defeated, "But let the record show you're a fucking asshole."

Uli was all smiles, jumping all the way over to her bestest friend and gave him a hug. "I'll allow it, I will allow it." Uli said.

As Uli and Ogun talked shop on the basic ins and outs of the matter at hand, Ted zoned out due to the three beers and the wizard lingo that flew over his head. He went cabinet by kitchen cabinet hunting for some snacks to even himself out. From the corner of his eye he noticed a void in the decoration of the trashed kitchen.

The two lizard looking fellows had disappeared from under the table.

"Gone! They're gone!" Ted whispered, annoyed the two spellslingers looked at him. He pointed under the table, and they knew immediately.

They alternated looking at each other, practicing the art of silently screaming towards your insides.

They scanned the kitchen in silence. Blood Fucker's tiny whiskers went razor straight. He let out a squeak, pointing his nose to the pantry, his little wings vibrating like a humming bird mid flight.

Perspiration and desperation added to the already congested

mix of smells floating around.

The twin roars of the human dragons broke the silence. Ted took one step towards the screen door before the scaled creatures bursted out the pantry, claws and teeth blazing in a sick green glow.

Blood Fucker reacted with protective instinct to his master and pounced towards the twin monster assault, Uli had the maternal twitch reaction to grab his fluffy tail before Blood Fucker became a dragon snack for the dragonsacks, she brought him to her chest and gripped him as to not allow anymore brazen heroics.

Ogun didn't have to think twice on what to do. Her branch covered wizard's staff leaped from its place next to the front door, she gripped it and barked out *"Chrotflint!"* as she snapped a branch off her wand.

Red wiggly runes spilled from the staff into the floor, calling upon the volcanic energy ever flowing through the planet, and evoked two blasts of volcanic rock akin to a couple of shells from a sawed off shotgun erupting right under the two fiends. They hit the ceiling hard and lit a flame, they crashed onto the floor, suits totally burned off revealing their whole bodies covered in the dragon scales.

"I thought they were dead! Screamed Uli. "Well they ain't!" yelled Ogun as she slipped the argonite knife out of her back pocket, "You two get out of here! Find Oman Zurr, bring the chosen one back and fix this mess of a world honey girl!" Ogun steadied herself, dizzy from the rebound of bringing forth such powerful magic.

"But, Aunt Ogun…"

The dragonsack twins saw through the ajar porch door the sword laying in the front yard emanating so much magic the other magic wielders in the room seemed like small potatoes. Now uninterested with the humans, they made a mad dash to get to the sword. Ogun broke another branch on her staff yelling *"Lazzon!"* a force field covered with red runes divided the room, sparks flew as the dragonsack's crashed into its magical wall.

"I'll catch up!" said Ogun, she gripped her wizard's staff with both hands facing the creatures who were winding up for another attack.

Ogun was a self taught wizard, the ancient schools were long gone. She trained in secret, developing her talent with the ever present fear of getting picked up by the police for practicing sorcery. But please do not misunderstand her ludic approach to the cosmic arts as half assed or amateurish. Yes, she was what you would call a "general practitioner," not having an attunement to a single branch of magic, opting for more of a Jack of all trades but master of none approach. It had been a while since she could go all out. But this was one of those do or die type of moments. There was a very present and probable thought that she could be on the losing end of the fight, it gave her a giddiness she long thought dead in her old age. She could put the volume to eleven for once, and it felt good.

Her adrenaline rush was cut short when she witnessed the scales on the dragonsack abominations flare up with a fluorescent crimson effulgence. The hundreds of runes dancing on the barrier wall sucked away into the dragonsacks.

"That's new!" Ogun said to herself. The tall lanky one opened its jaws and belched out dragon fire. The vertically impaired one followed suit, but instead of wild chaotic flame, a laser focused plasma shot out its bile soaked mouth. Ogun ducked under what was left of her force field, the flame curling her hair to a crisp, the beam of fire carving a line horizontally on her now burning home.

Ogun beckoned back the runes from the shield spell to her staff.

"*Zyclon!*" she yelled, breaking another small branch. The runic symbols whirled into two human sized tornadoes. the freaks may be able to feed on magic, but she wanted to make it hurt.

The tiny tornadoes which sucked up every sharp kitchen appliance could at least give them a nasty paper cut, and boy howdy, did they ever. Her vision blurred, keeping balance an effort at this point, consecutive spells causing the dreaded magical rebound that no sorcerer was a fan of.

The dragonsack boys screeched from the barrage of blenders and toaster ovens smashing into their bodies.

The tornadoes died, pulled into the dragonsack twins for another fiery salvo.

Ogun was on her way to be magically tapped out, she raised the argonite blade to a ready position.

She felt the heat from the twin flamed attack, she couldn't help but grin.

13

"Gunther and Olaff"

Uli raced her way to the car, Ted dragged the sword behind him leaving a trail of split dirt deep enough to plant full grown trees.

Explosions and structural damage sounding off behind their escape. Their only savior from a duo of living nightmares was the one aunt that always got black out drunk and would hit on Ted during the winter holidays.

BOOM! KRAKOOM! the screen door exploded off its hinges, Aunt Ogun rolled out into her front yard, fire engulfing the edges of her thrift store ensemble. Her staff smoking next to her, she reached around her landing site for the argonite knife, now lost under the mess of leaves.

"Aunt Ogun!" Uli was about to dash back to aunt.

"I'm okay Hun! Keep going, I'm having a ball over here!"

The dragon twins crawled out of the hole where the screen door once stood. Their scales glowed red inhaling the fires back into their body.

The tall one (let's call him Gunther) closed his eyes as he concentrated the reabsorbed fire magic into his throat, a wave of steel melting flames flew forth, heading right for Ogun.

"Noooooo!" Screamed Uli, her arm stretched out, focusing her mind into a couple of words.

"Hosto Hilak!"

Dead leaves gathered around Ogun, moving her away from the blast.

Pride filled Ogun's battle exhausted body "Hah! DEAD leaves, clever girl."

The short dragonsack (let's call the short one Olaff) looked at Uli like a coked out meerkat that just located its next fix. Olaff saw an aura on Uli that was faint but resembled black ink floating in water.

"Shit...Uli! Turn the spell off, you just ratted yourself out!"

Olaff roared. razor nailed feet charging at Uli.

"I'm sorry old friend," Ogun said as she placed her right knee in the middle of her staff *"Shere Vorte!"* The staff bursted in two, two giant runic symbols leapt from the broken pieces landing on top of Gunther and Olaff pinning them to the ground. They squirmed and squealed from the pain of manifested magic words dropping on them like led weighted meteors.

Ted threw Uli in the passenger seat as easily as he would his backpack.

"We have to help her!" Uli cried. Ted had started the car and punched it, the car then reminded Ted that he did not know how to drive stick by stalling the engine. Uli kicked open her door ready to die in battle next to Ogun.

Ted pushed his arm to pin her to the seat "She's buying us time! Let her do her thing, honor her wish dammit! Now switch with me!" Uli bit, scratched and fought against Ted's surprisingly heavy arm, but it didn't budge.

"Fine! Move!" tears running from her eyes, they tumbled over each other switching places. She kicked the car in gear and ripped out of the blazing battle.

Uli watched as her aunt's house became smaller in the rear view mirror, all she could do was run away and cry, in that moment feeling more like a useless child than a life saving Necromancer.

Ogun ruined her staff and was magically empty at that point, but she at least got the sword, Uli and Ted out of there.

The scales on the dragonsack twins glowed once more, the giant runes slowly losing structure, morphing to a static energy ready to be consumed, it would only be a matter of time before they'd be free and fully charged. She grabbed the remains of her staff and charged at Olaff and Gunther. The last of the weight runes absorbed, fire would soon come, age took people in their beds, at home or hospice with a lack of fanfare most unbecoming to Ogun, this had spectacle and class, this had a weight to it, this will do for her last stand. Because to her, leaving should be done the same way you got here, kicking and screaming.

14

"Silent Ride"

Ted, Uli and B.F. drove the back roads in absolute silence, all three staring out the windshield in a post traumatic haze. Uli and Ted's psyche was busy boxing up everything that had transpired to later be dumped in the deepest corner of their subconscious, so it must be forgiven that neither noticed they took the wrong exit into a back road that was under serious repairs since last year's hurricane season.

Ted clocked back into reality first, the road became composed of large gravel and potholes, bouncing the car up and down like an off-road course.

"Uli, Ulzz, Uli," Ted looked at her for the first time in hours, Uli's eyes dry and bloodshot, she had forgotten how to blink since Ogun's home.

Ted, with his wits fully online, saw what they were driving to, a dead end sign, with a chasm behind said sign for good measure. "Uli, slow down dude, Uli…"

Where was Uli mentally? Though going under the speed limit, their speed would guarantee either breaking their necks on the security wall placed before the bridge, or falling to their doom.

Blood Fucker tried to help running around Uli's shoulders, biting her ears every lap he took. They survived a mutant attack in the woods, Ted was not ready to go out by way of a hole in the ground.

With an "I'm so sorry," and a "Please don't hate me," Ted opted for what they lovingly called the emergency button.

He gave her a wet willy.

She grabbed her ear and screamed in disgust, tears and snot covering her face, she wondered why she was so rudely taken out of her own private la la land "What the shit Ted?! A fucking wet willy?" Ted grabbed her by the hair and raised her eyes to the oncoming wall of warning signs.

"Pump the breaks!"

The tires screamed a concerto of burnt rubber and wasted breaks until the ratty old car came to a halt.

"What the hell is wrong with you!?"

"Sorry," Uli said, "Had one of those clean up sessions in my noggin, must have spaced out."

"Oh you think!?" as much as he loved and understood Uli's unique little quirks, he was dealing with his own inner turmoil.

"So NOW we call the cops?" Ted asked.

"Are you crazy? Aunt Ogun is a witch, if the police go there and find all that magic crap all over the place they'll put her in jail!"

"Only if she's alive though, right?" Ted said, milliseconds too late to realize how much of an insensitive goober he is.

"Yeah thanks Ted, IF she's alive, totally right."

Uli wanted to go back and save her dearest Aunt. But like it or not Ogun set the board in such a way as to get them out of there with at least a minor amount of a head start. And the path was clear, well, clear-ish anyway.

"Aunt Ogun sacrificed herself so we could go on a quest." Uli said.

"Uli please, Ogun got caught or, um, the other not so nice thing, we have to go to the cops now, or like lay low for like a week, or five years, I don't know, this has gotten out of our hands by way too much man."

"No!" she said, with the authority of a soccer mom that moonlights as the chieftain of a barbarian horde.

"But why!?" he said, stretching that "why" out long enough to annoy even himself on the delivery. If only for a second, his frustration and anxiety poked out strong enough for Uli to physically and verbally move away from him.

"Why does it have to be us? Just because this piece of shit destroyed my car, and then you and your aunt can't help wanting to live out some fantasy more at home a million years ago?"

"The world needs us?"

"No it does not! I mean, it's not so bad is it?"

Uli wanted to have something locked and loaded to fire for such a conformist comment, but she was out of ammo.

"Look, maybe you're right, but the world is broken Teddy and you know it. And we have the one thing that could kick it back on the rails, isn't it our responsibility to use it?."

"But it's not even a prophecy" Ted said, while rubbing the headache that was revving up between his eyes.

"If you only wait for prophecies or holy decrees to do the right thing dude, you'll end up not doing shit your whole life don't you think?"

Ted got a five second brain freeze trying to wrap his head around that disturbingly eloquent comment.

"If I could do this alone I would, I know you don't like this type of stuff, but that's why I threw down the Ozen Maloique," Ted cringed at the naming of the super secret promise.

Uli sat looking at the unbuilt bridge up ahead, having to kick away the poetic analogy that the image was provoking in her.

Ted was tired, they all were, he looked at Uli petting Blood Fucker as the little guy tried to console her. She just lost a loved one and now has a target on her back, and she still wants to go on with it. Ted knew no such resolve, or that will power bull poop his manager Mark would throw up about. Every bone in his body wanted to go home and call it quits, and he knew that even if he did, Uli would crawl on without him, just to see what the quest could bring, and then probably get killed, and then he would live the rest of his life guilt ridden that he didn't help.

"So, are we going or what?" Ted said with a defeated twang to it.

Uli was reminded why she called Ted her best friend.

15

"Secrets"

President Volshtadt sat on a throne of the darkest of onyx, the enormous chair was set up on the highest spot of his mansion/castle/capitol building, pointing out at the city that stood as the crown jewel to his dominion.

As a meditative exercise, he would sit and look back on his life in perfect chronological order, as to constantly remind himself what it took to get here.

The long game of subjugation, the snail crawls towards adapting humanity to bend the knee, not through force, but by time and sheer boredom. Kalammet and Volshtadt dedicated every second of every moment to building the machine that would swallow the world whole.

Every calculation, every act of kindness, every act of horrific brutality, each one a cog moving the goal forward, if even by an inch.

This all started with that cursed accident, how something so stupid was the catalyst to how the world is now has always fascinated Volshtadt. Hero, villain, scholar, dumb ass, all play a part in the building of tomorrow, whether they like their role in it or not.

It was always understood that Volshtadt would (and should) lose. The only thing needed was some deranged soul to speak of vision and prophecy, that's all it took and humanity would drink it like medicine. So simple, light vs. dark, here take some shiny swords, go at it kids.

When the unthinkable happened, he and Kalammet embraced the opportunity. But ever since that day, his immortal eyes have seen the horizon for so long that despite all the so called progress, he couldn't help but feel that the world began to rot from the inside out.

The smallest, most subtle of smiles appeared on his face. He didn't know why, didn't know how, but for the first time in a very long time, he felt he was in danger.

A tension constricted his chest, his jaw stiffened and his brain reopened a room in him that had not been visited for millennia, his true self, action and reaction, attack and defend, kill or be killed.

Despite his immortal intellect, he found comfort in the binary nature of nature itself.

It was clean, pure, and most of all, it was damn fun.

A sensation was poking him in the ribs playfully saying "Uh oh, somebody is picking a fight. It was about damn time."

"Please do not slither in so silently wizard, It makes me feel old and unable to read your presence," said Volshtadt, sounding like a dad that just woke up from a nap.

"Apologies, you called for me?"

"Yes, I've been curious about what you found out about the anomaly you mentioned this morning, did your dragon pets find the glitch?"

Kalammet hesitated for a half a second. "Yes they did, they located the anomaly a few hours south of the capitol, a cursed wine bottle was found and uncorked, some poor soul drank its contents, if the curse didn't kill him the spoiled wine did, nothing to worry about."

Volshtadt let the answer hang in the air for a moment.

"Is something the matter?"

"I have been feeling a bit off if I'm being honest." Volshtadt confessed.

"Off ?"

"Not myself, or actually more like myself," Volshtadt pondered while scratching the back of his neck. "I've been here for too long, It's hard to pin down who you are after so long, one of these many side effects of immortality I suppose," he let out a chuckle that Kalammet felt forced to join in on.

"Eternity has its shortcomings, yes."

Neither spoke, the silence stretching longer and longer,

Kalammet knew he was in dangerous territory, his King and creation was fishing.

The eyes of the drakenstatz are perpetually tethered to Kalammet, feeding him surveillance while capturing any mystic practitioner or magical object his dragon grafted bloodhounds could locate. When two of his creatures (Olaff and Gunther) woke up from their bout with the witch from the Scatter Lands, he saw with his borrowed eyes the Dammerung, back from its forced exile in the forever of space. Not only was it back, but on the move.

Aiden long dead and magic dwindling as it is, it served no

alarm to him, until he saw the girl and the floating miasma of her affinity gathered around her, a cursed Necromancer!

No sooner than the wave of live feed of bad news took over his mind, President Volshtadt called him up for a debriefing.

Kalammet felt compelled for a moment to inform Volshtadt, but telling the once Voidlord of components of his past coming back to Thira caused him hesitation. The Forlen Empire prevailed, Thira moved on, they all did, and the return of ancient pieces of a failed prophecy could set in motion things he would prefer left derelict. He did not enjoy lying to his ruler, but Kalammet did like the depressed but malleable husk Volshtadt had become, having him revert to his old barbaric self in these more civilized eras would be hard to manage to say the least.

Though not blessed with tapping into ley lines or having dragons for eyes, Volshtadt still was the single most powerful source of condensed magic in the realm, his aura so powerful to the ebb and flow of energies, he had to have noticed the disturbance even before Kalammet informed him.

But he didn't know it was Dammerung, and Kalammet aimed to keep it that way, for the good of the empire, for the sanity of his king, and mostly because he worked too long and to hard to have a sword and a dead prince come and trash what took him thousands of lifetimes to get just right.

"So, a cursed wine bottle?"

"Yes."

"Are you sure?"

There it is, the line cast out into the lake once more, Kalammet had to think well and quick to conjure up a lie far more convincing than any spell he's produced as of late.

"Sire, you think me a liar? Have I ever kept things from you?

Why would I do so on some lowly cursed libation? If need be I shall find said bottle and place it before your feet. But with all respect, I find your lack of belief a bit disrespectful."

The floor shook with the force of a small earthquake, Volshtadt's throne turning an incandescent red, his jaw locked low to his neck in a feline predatory stare, neither averting their eyes.

Volshtadt did feel gratitude to his maker, mixed with a tiny pinch of resentment of bringing him into existence in the first place. But the old magical fart was useful.

The rumble lulled to a stop.

"I'm sorry, life has been a bit dull as of late, you cannot blame a man for hoping for some excitement from time to time." Volshtadt said with a gambler's smile, inviting yet threatening in tandem. He didn't mean the apology, and he wanted the warlock to know it.

"No apology needed, I understand."

"I think I'll be going to bed soon."

"Of course."

Kalammet made his way out.

Volshtadt stayed in silence, amused at his childishness. As if waiting for his parents to go to bed, he pushed himself out of his throne and went to a hidden fridge in the wall, he pulled out a cheap brand of beer, guzzled it down with the pleasure of a blue collar worker after a long day of work. He looked out into the city, a plethora of things were eating him from the inside. His most trusted advisor was keeping something from him, a deep, quiet heat crawled inside his mind, and he couldn't help but feel that they were both connected.

16

"Luminous Lakes Mall"

The late afternoon sun hung heavy in the sky by the time Uli, Ted and B.F. made it to the supposed location of the tomb of one of the original founders of Necromancy.

They were not confronted by a soul stealing necropolis, they got the next worst thing, a mall. Luminous Lakes Mall, never will you find a place with such treachery and villainy, and really big birthday cake sized chocolate chip cookies.

"Maybe it's like a huge glamour spell or something," Uli said as a young couple walked next to them with a baby in a stroller, all three holding corn dogs the size of the infants whole body.

"If it's a glamour shot or whatever, it's a damn good one."

"Don't be a smart ass Ted, it doesn't fit you."

"I'm not, come on dude, you can smell the corn dogs."

She took a whiff just to shut Ted up and yes, corn dogs, damn good smelling corn dogs at that.

"What do we do with the sword? We can't leave it here and we can't just bring it into a public area, it's a bit of a conversation starter isn't it?"

"No worries dude, all these places have those cheap fantasy knockoff sword stores, if anything this is the one place we can walk around freely with it."

"Fine, but keep yourself and Blood Fucker away from it, we don't want it turning on and pulling a Pasta Barn incident."

Ted ripped out the already faulty seat belts and made a strap to carry Dammerung on his back. Despite not working out, he had a default level of strength equal to any protein chugging gym rat, yet the sword's weight still felt like he had a gorilla using him for the world's worst piggy back ride.

* * *

Corn dogs in hand, they decided to get a lay of the land. They scouted the goth store known as "The Vampire Coffin" in the hopes to find a backdoor, or talking gargoyle, or even a pathway to another dimension, but no such luck. just a new eye shadow brand Uli had been looking for everywhere.

They went to the crystal shop and again nothing.

Next that one store that smells like a gaggle of grandmas making potpourri bags, nothing. They walked the whole complex twice over and no sign of the once foreboding tomb.

They took a seat at the newly renovated common area at the center of Luminous Lakes to let Ted get the hunk of dimensional steel off of him and allow his spine to stop screaming in hellish agony.

The only thing remotely terrifying in this center of commerce was a five year old demon spawn of a child some tired mom unleashed on the fun zone play area, his reign of fury involved many a toddler vanishing to the ball pit.

Blood Fucker shifted inside Uli's bag as he took his late afternoon nap after feasting on some sugar packets his master had saved a while ago.

"He's like a wizard pet thing. He could be our necromancy detector right?" Ted asked, pointing at Uli's bag.

Uli liked the idea, but an undead woodland rodent would attract too much attention.

"We gotta wait till everybody's gone, then see if the little guy can scratch something up."

"Yeah but where are we gonna hide until then?"

Uli and Ted made the third jog around the mall to find a suitable place to lay low until they close the place down.

Like many shopping centers, they have less circulated halls than others, you know the ones, the establishments shunned by polite society, the aforementioned knockoff sword and knife stores, the comic and trading card shops that catered to children and man-children alike. Though not particularly dangerous, normal everyday people and security alike would avoid strolling these geek infested spaces.

There they found a long line of kiosks with empty display cases put together in a manner for the vendor to stand in the middle and try to overcharge you for cheap cologne or a novelty hat.

Some of the regulars in the area saw them sneak into the kiosk closest to the bathroom, but didn't really care to sound the alarm, shrugging it off as two perverts just about to get their jollies in the least romantic spot in the mall, because love makes a many passionate souls commit to lust in the oddest of places, and also because some people are just horny like that.

17

"Tomb Sniffer"

The last giant cookie sold and the final coin spent in the local arcade. The lights were dimmed and the majority of the shops put down their steel gates for the night.

Uli and company came out of hiding into the dormant shopping center. When a place who's daily energy is that of controlled chaos and teenage boosted capitalism, its now silent and sterile stillness gave the place a malevolent, foreboding essence, and being locked in behind its sliding doors added to the sensation of being stuck in a jail, or dare I say dungeon, (low hanging fruit I know, but the metaphor was right there, and you would have judged me more harshly if I hadn't pointed it out. You know it to be true).

"Cool," was Uli's first review of her surroundings. The growing necromantic aura within her couldn't help but feel a bit more at home in such a poorly lighted liminal space.

Now that the living were gone for the day, Uli could feel a mystical pull while being in the building, but B.F. was made of pure undead arcane energy, he felt more of a magnetic current dragging him to a point of origin, rotted magic is the un-life force of the dead, and B.F. could finally smell it.

They followed the little guy for most of an hour, stopping briefly to let their resident dead guy detector eat a half eaten pizza he found.

They took a couple of pee breaks at the designated restrooms, which were as always situated next to the emergency exits and service doors.

Neither Ted or Uli washed their hands (barbarism) as they exited the bathroom they came out to find B.F. scratching at the service door. They opened it for the little guy who immediately zipped over to a wall at the end of the door covered hall. Both of the humans present felt like morons. What? The entrance to a prison tomb was just gonna be at the pizza place or that useless tech store with all the recliners? shame on you two.

If the Mall had the dungeon vibe down, the service corridors had the catacomb essence down to perfection.

Blood Fucker scratched like a dog wanting out to potty, the sense of purpose of helping his master gave him a well deserved taste of pride.

Even Uli's modest amount of magic talent could see the ink like miasma coming off the wall. Thick, stagnant smoke-like clouds clung to the beige drywall, staining it with a decayed outer layer. She could feel it, the invasive smoke invisible to non magic users trigger a part of her brain that despite being attuned to this power, couldn't help but speak up and say, "What are you doing here Uli? You dumb delusional little girl, you're dealing with dark demonic forces!"

The hair on their necks slowly rose, catching the cold beads of sweat manifesting on their skin, letting the human meat bags know they are approaching something they shouldn't.

Blood Fucker's palpable enthusiasm to help Uli was just too cute to her eyes. She had only spent a short amount of time with her familiar, but she was happy that it was able to develop a personality that was amicable, thank the gods he wasn't like a world class jerk that ate people's faces or anything of the sort.

Ted summoned his love for cop movies and shoulder rammed the wall a couple of times, but all he managed to do was dent the drywall, whatever behind it being as solid as cement.

They pondered getting tools from a store in the mall, but hardware like that isn't typically found next to the massage shop. They put Blood Fucker on the sword and hoped it would plow into the wall, but no luck since it started its way in the opposite direction.

"Use some of that dead people super joojoo stuff," Ted said, now more exasperated than fearful.

"Necromancy is not a KABOOM kind of magic Ted, more a unleash the dead to spit acid and eat you kind of magic."

A black light of an idea flickered into life over Uli, and the way she stared at B.F. made him happy but also scared for his un-life. Nobody living or otherwise has a good time throwing up, throwing up acid? even less so.

She gently lifted him, "B.F. we need ya buddy," the squirrel nodded nervously, "And I don't want you to do something you don't wanna do."

"Oh, so the squirrel gets a choice?!" Ted protested.

"Shush," Uli put her attention back on B.F. "But I need ya to shoot up some of that acid puke of yours on the wall, could you do that for me?"

B.F. didn't hesitate, ramming his whole left arm down his mouth to provoke the green acid to come up. He dry heaved a couple of times, by the third false start, the fluorescent green liquid shot from his tiny face. Uli wielded him like a little squirt gun and doused the thick wall before them.

The smell of sulfur and pizza stained the air, Ted was two heaves from gagging himself.

The paint peeled off, the cement and ancient stone disintegrated with a boiling hiss.

Uli gave herself a mental pat on the back, she brought back from the dead the pocket sized hellion that made that level of a mess. The poisonous fumes dissipated, revealing a hole into pitch black nothing.

Wind moaned out of the smoking crevice, as if the catacomb itself was allowed to breathe once more. Its icy breath smelled of damp rock and stale oils as ancient as Thira itself.

"Good job Blood Fucker! Who's my acid pumping little soldier?" Uli said, B.F. tired and spent squeaked in glee.

Uli poked her head in, a magic sensor within the darkness was triggered by her presence, the infinite staircase within then lit up, gelatinous oil sitting in two canals on each side of the staircase emanated the dancing light providing the illumination for all who dared to enter.

Sporting Blood Fucker on her shoulder, Uli slid through into the hole. She made her way down, Ted made like an anchor and did not move an inch. Not so much paralyzed by fear, more like his brain didn't know what to do next.

"What's wrong? Get your butt in gear you big boob, let's

go!"

Uli acted like she was on her way to her favorite theme park. Nobody should be this happy to go into what looked like the waiting room to the underworld. Ted found her enthusiasm disturbing, he looked back to the service corridor leading to the shopping mall, "Fuck me right?"

"What?" Uli asked.

"I said FUCK ME right?"

"Oh Ted we've talked about this, it would just make things strange between us," Uli said sympathetically. Ted snorted and allowed a grin as he squeezed over to the staircase. "Oh yeah, you're right, plus who am I to make you break your vow of purity."

"I AM NOT A VIRGIN!" Uli objected.

"Uli, it's okay, being a virgin was only a stigma in high school, as an adult it's just sad," Ted said as they both made their way down the stone stairwell to meet a Necromancer.

18

"Carl Weatherson"

Mother was on her way to drop off Carl at work, the Weatherson home can only afford one car and Mama Weatherson needs it later for her date. Carl was thirty two, dark of skin, five pounds heavier than his build was made for, divorced and now playing roommate to his very tired, but very loving mother.

Carl traced a circle and line over his chest, this was to enact the connection of man to the supreme sun, a gesture to honor his faith to the goddess of light and justice, Etheria.

He grabbed his lunch box, kissed his mom goodbye and walked through the revolving doors of the Luminous Lakes Mall. For he not only worked there, but was the protector of peace, the guardian of order, the sentinel of stoic justice to this center of commerce. He was the night shift mall cop!

He waved to all the clerks and managers as he walked by the multiple shops and stands, all who worked at Luminous Lakes loved Carl.

Perhaps love is a strong word, tolerated was more accurate, he was nice enough and eager to serve and protect, having the highest record of shoplifters caught as well as the reigning champion of helping many an old folk with their bags.

But he just couldn't help it, sooner or later, one way or another, he would ask a customer, "Have you found the light of Etheria in your heart?" or, "Has Etheria gifted you the new light today?" or the ever popular "I see a little bit of Etheria in you, would you like more?"

The rock that broke the golem's back happened two weeks ago when a young lady by the name of Rina Pippner accidentally left an unpaid lipstick in her pocket as she passed through the sensor of the cosmetics store. The alarm wailed on, calling to Carl as if a damsel in distress, he saw the unaware perpetrator walk to the exit, ignoring the blaring alarm, Ms. Pippner was much too enthralled by the hot gossip of her friend Amanda cheating on Devin that one time behind that burger joint during the spring fling prom.

Carl's love for the light of Etheria and justice is absolute, but when the long arm of the law must strike, said long arm has a hard time measuring its strength. The combination of adrenaline and the opportunity to deal out divine punishment on the wicked made Carl charge into Rina Pippner exclaiming "Shoplifter, stop in the name of the law!"

The tackle was bad enough, he then proceeded to perform a suplex on the high school student. The only thing that saved him from being kicked out of a job and into a prison was that the young Rina, though honestly forgetting the lipstick in her pocket, also apparently forgot to pay for the three tops, two summer dresses and facial skin care kit she stuffed in her large pink purse.

His boss, who to this day Carl insists on calling the "Captain" gave him the final warning to not badger or cripple the customers, because it was against the law. Carl would never infringe on such sacred words, but the laws of Etheria are greater and older, the mall cop not one who enjoys troubling others, he promised all the same, Mama Weatherson wants this month's rent paid on time.

**

He scanned the perimeter and saw nothing out of the ordinary, stepped into the security office, punched his card, and prepared for the day's battle.

Carl strapped on his utility belt, sheathed his heavy metal flashlight known as the *Skullbuster 3000*, then double checked the safety lock on the pepper spray, and finally tapped the taser to hear the ever menacing yet pleasing *BZZZZZT!*

He went to the bathroom, closed the door and gave himself a good look in the mirror, even though being the simple uniform of a mall security guard, Carl felt purpose through every thread of the cheap polyester blend. He pulled some paper towels out of the dispenser and placed them on the floor, perfectly situating them to serve as the landing spots for his knees. He pulled from his pocket an amulet, a silver disk in the shape of an oval that fit in his palm perfectly, on its face was a simple carving of a circle and a line going from top to bottom, the sign of Etheria, Goddess of light and creation.

He grasped it with both hands and broke into prayer "Etheria was, Etheria is, Etheria will be, light guides, light protects, her light sees all evil threats, I her sword, I her shield, in her light the darkness sealed! Guide me tonight oh holy mother, so I may guide to your light another."

There he knelt in silence, as if waiting for his goddess to finally say something. Regrettably the only sound that was present was an ambush of a flatulence dispensed by one Evan Gonk who was in one of the stalls Carl forgot to check.

"Carl, you know you're not allowed to do that at work..."

"Fair enough, do YOU know you're not allowed to keep the shoplifted merchandise?"

Evan stayed silent for a beat "Fair enough." he let out one more earth rumbling toot which made Carl seriously consider doing his late afternoon prayer somewhere else.

He made it to the main hall of the mall and started his first round around his beat. He walked ruler straight with a gate in his step that looked more like a march than a casual walk.

Eyes scanning every corner, customer and employee about. Every ounce of data scrolled down in his internal evidence book.

-Brayden at the shoe store changed his haircut to cover his bald spot.

-That old couple sat in the food court ten minutes past the allotted time without eating anything.

-The child hurling smaller kids into the ball pit must be dealt with.

-Kimberly at Spandex Hut looked at me, could be flirting, could be disdain, investigate later.

He may not be protecting the streets from thugs, or saving kids from burning buildings, but by Etheria and the memory of his passed father, he was going to make sure every man, woman and child felt safe within the hallowed halls of Luminous Lakes Mall.

His "Captain" appreciated how Carl took his job, and understood that every now and then you were going to get a religious nut on the payroll, it was inevitable, but the constant complaints from the regulars forced the good Captain to put Carl on the late shift, which involved patrolling the last few hours of the stores being opened, then double checking the mall before closing, and finally serving as the night security for the entirety of the building, less people meant less targets to tackle.

It was now closing time and the crowds of consumers made their way home, Carl didn't mind working alone at night. As depressing as it might sound, he had grown accustomed to solitude as of recently, the divorce to "She who shall not be named" hit him hard, he was madly in love with her, and she knew well his devotion to Etheria and his mother, but it was obvious to all around them that "She who shall not be named" would always be third place in Carl's heart and soul.

The holy man couldn't help it, his obsessive worship made him unwanted company to all close to him. One would think that a life of clergy would be the right fit for him, but the church of Etheria much like the rest of the history of Thira was vaguely present or near extinct, the remnants of this wayward faith is followed now in private.

As the stores closed and the revolving doors locked, it was time for Carl's mandatory lunch break, he didn't like it, saying that, "food only slows me down during the job, having an empty belly keeps my senses sharp," but the higher ups obligated him out of union code as to not bring about possible lawsuits in the future.

"CARL WEATHERSON"

Lunch box in hand he went to his favorite spot in the whole mall, with its glass dome that during the day would let the natural light come in. But at night when most of the lights were off, it gave a lovely view of the starry night sky.

Mrs. Weatherson's signature triple decker sandwiches and tar black coffee were always the perfect combo while he did his best to recognize the constellations his father long ago pointed out to him. Telling him they were the eyes of the angels of Etheria, making sure we were safe.

The tap, tap, tap of a far off skitter interrupted his moment of union obligated peace. It was coming from what he called the, "dark side of the mall" quadrant. His gut, training and eagerness for a perpetrator bolted him hop up instantly unleashing his Skullbuster flashlight, the two foot monstrosity could illuminate the very void itself, and the weight and construction of it was tailor made to make sure if Carl needed to help a evil doer see the light of Etheria, he was going to see it with extreme prejudice.

He placed his free hand on his belt to quiet its merry jingle jangle and silently made his way down the mall.

19

"Hot on the trail"

Carl reached a far off kiosk where clearly some perps hid away till the mall closed, a clever ploy that angered Carl for not noticing it earlier, but the eyes of justice have to blink from time to time. He turned the flashlight off to not alert of his presence.

He thought to himself, "Thieves obviously, or some punks trying to vandalize the fur store on the rich side of the mall."

He crouched and went from one decorative fern to another using his eagle eyes now accustomed to the darkened halls of the shopping center.

Carl thought he was dealing with professionals, every time he would reach a corner of the mall, he would hear the shuffle of feet come from the other side of the complex. "They're trying to shake me off their tail, not tonight kids, not tonight."

Much to the dismay of Carl's feet, this went on for the better part of an hour, for the life of him he just couldn't find them. If the Captain would have heeded his recommendation of repairing the security cameras he wouldn't be playing cat and mouse with what seemed to be ghosts with annoyingly squeaky sneakers. He stopped at a water fountain to hydrate and catch his breath, he's not the young buck he was a mere few years ago, he could practically hear his long forgotten gym membership laugh its laminated face off from the comfort of his nylon wallet.

He was failing the badge, worst of all he was failing the good name of his fallen father Officer Jacob Weatherson, the dog pile of shame was heavy, but if Carl had something in spades it was his capacity to rally, he cracked his neck, his back, his shoulders and looked back at the maze like structure of Luminous Lakes, "Unlucky for you rats, this cat is hungry, hungry for justi...Ouch!"

Carl felt as if someone tried to brand him with a hot poker on his chest, the amulet glowed under his thick uniform shirt. Though alarmed he took the time to unbutton the shirt and pull out the now shining symbol of Etheria. he pulled it away enough to stop the burn and got a good look at it.

Words left him, mouth and eyes wide with awe. Vindication, wonder, fear, this trinity of concepts flooded his brain to the brim. The one thing he wanted his whole life happened, in front of a senior citizen store that was having a special on soft cushioned toilet seats, Carl had received a sign.

"Etheria, what do you wish of me?"

The light dimmed in the relic, almost turning off completely. "Nonononono wait, hold on a second wait, come on now!" he paced around in a panic till the light returned in an instant the moment he made his way to the south hall "There we go! There we go!"

It dimmed again, only to light up again the further he went down the south hall.

His concentration somewhere else, he rammed into a granite pot holding a fake palm tree. It hurt him plenty, but the excitement spark of adrenaline from miracle boosted jewelry kept him from even noticing his scratched knees and bloodied trousers.

The light shined brighter and brighter with every step towards the restrooms, he could feel his corneas burning by the time he made it to the ajar service door. He peeked in enough to see a hole at the end of the corridor, smoke fuming off of the human size opening, the amulet pulsed with urgent repetitive cycles.

"Destruction of private property. Heathens!"

20

"The Near Infinite Staircase to the dead guy who's gonna help Uli bring back the Chosen One and stuff"

As they made their way down to the ancient storage space for dead people, statues adorned the channels of fire leading down. Long eroded stone men and women averting their eyes in horror to whatever was below.

"Why are they looking away?"

"Fear? Shame? I don't know dude, I mean, Necromancers aren't what you would call historically loved throughout the land."

Alchemists with their fancy equipment, Druids with their menagerie of beasts to shapeshift in, Hydromancers and their water fountain antics were held in high regard. But you desecrate a few graves and defile a few cadavers and now you're a menace to magic society.

"This guy down here, was important and scary enough to build this for him, but hated enough to make sure the permanent decor was designed to offend and shun him, even in death. Must have been a *sunnafabitch*," Uli deduced.

Ted and Uli's knees began to complain, neither being track and field stars. They would look back every now and then from the morbid reflex of reminding themselves that if they made it out alive, it was gonna suck balls to climb their way up.

"It's been thousands of years since he died right? There can't be enough to work with," Ted said.

Uli went on without answering, Ted wasn't wrong, but incantations such as the one stored in the copper tube gifted to them by Ogun only exist if they can be used, if the subject of the incantation doesn't exist, the scroll would just crumble away from existence, meaning that, if the text is on these pages, they can still be used.

The old super wizards back in the day pumped so much magic into these one time use spells to bypass any need of skill. Only requirement was knowing how to read it, with an added bonus of no magic rebound to put you in the hospital.

After twenty minutes and two sit down breaks they made it to the end of the damn staircase.

They looked at the million stairs behind them and did a quiet high five relishing the silent victory of actually making it. For underachievers, every little win is meant to be savored to its maximum potential. It's the little things, for Ted and Uli and their kind in the world, it's the only things they got most of the time.

The flammable jelly guided them to a massive vault-like door sporting eight key holes of multiple sizes, dozens of gears and rusted cogs interconnected around the intricately decorated door depicting large godly figures eating humans by the fistful. That behemoth of a door would have been a quest killer right there, had someone remembered to lock it before leaving.

"People were short back then huh?" Ted said as his head bumped into the low ceiling of the main burial room, Even Uli had to crouch a bit. The place was shaped like a pentacle. Runes, long forgotten words and a hoarder's wet dream of religious artefacts overrun every edge of the hidden room.

At the five corners of the room on some very intricate pedestals lay in display five chests.

Uli's essence resonated with the final resting chamber, to other magic sensitives, this place felt and smelled like a predator's den, to her, a cozy cabin in the woods filled with books and hot cocoa.

They looked at the boxes at a safe distance. They had seen enough movies and read enough fiction to know, ancient assholes loved putting traps in things and places like this. Once the gods of paranoia were pleased and Uli felt out to see if any booby was trapped, she gave the okay to look inside, they opened the boxes to find skeletal remains, each skeletal appendage tucked into their very snug containers. They looked for the one containing Oman Zurr's head, once opened the skull was yellowed but well kept, covered in ancient writing from a bygone language.

"Well, now what?" Ted asked.

Uli pulled the copper tube out, popping the cap and gently removing the weathered parchment paper.

"I say the words and we should have a revived Necromancer."

"Hurry up dude, not to be a buzz kill, but I would prefer to not be underground with dead things as long as we have."

She nodded, "So I just say the words, throw away, easy peasy."

Uli rolled open the paper, getting a good look at the writings in the scroll. A gust of wind flew through the burial room as if by cue, the fire jelly illuminating the area was close to flickering out of existence as well. Spells and incantations don't have to do such flashy fanfare, but any wizard worth his salt has a taste for theatrics. What's the fun of having the raw sources of creation bend to your will if you can't make it have some panache.

She went to the center altar, placed the skull on it and read the words out loud, the incantations were neatly spelled and double spaced for good measure, making even its arcane words easy to read. It felt almost like it was designed so any idiot could use it. Fine by Uli, less work is good work. The ancient words sounding like a panicked mandrill drowning on force fed pudding.

Her voice took on an echo, way too big for the room they're in. She turned and smiled at Ted scrunching up her arms and committing to a series of excited hops. He gave her a quick nervous smile and waved his hand in the "hurry the fuck up" fashion. She playfully frowned and went back to it. Time is a factor when using these things, and losing too much of the general flow of the words can render it useless. The jelly flames grew higher, the dance between green and yellow tones flashed into cobalt black fire, its edges producing a dark undulating blue.

The skull vibrated, a black ooze manifested, lashing out to each box with tentacles made of the thick miasma of death magic. The spell was close to completion, the scroll slowly catching fire, words glowed as they burned off the thick faded scroll.

Modernity has forgotten when a word is put to paper it is now properly a tangible concept. Proving with this simple act that writing is magic, a thing in the infinite void, formless and without name, is shaped into something, transfused to reality.

Uli's eyes, teeth and lips stained in the ebony substance signature to her magical attunement.

A scream sounding like thousands of nails scratching a warehouse worth of chalkboards shook the catacomb. Ted and Uli's body ached at the assault to the ears. The high pitched explosion morphed into a cackle, fading several octaves to an actual human voice. Even Uli felt more like shitting her pants than jumping in joy of pulling off the one shot revival spell.

The demonic laugh went three minutes too long, they went from scared, to confused, to just annoyed.

"Um, Mr. Skull Sir, could you please stop doing that?" Uli asked, but the laughing cranium kept on keeping on.

"Hey! Shut it already!" Uli shot out, the skull hushed from the first reprimand in all his living and dead existence.

His eyes lit with sapphire red, Ted avoiding eye contact at all cost, because, well, it seems prudent to be honest here.

The possessed head let out a few yips and then spoke a language not heard in Thira for a good long while. Unintelligible as it was, it was clear that he was not happy.

"Skull sir, we can't understand at all what you're saying."

The words surprised him, intrigued by what Uli said. It mumbled a few things to himself, sparking his eyes to go emerald green, Uli's eyes locked on to the pretty colors and Ted witnessed a thick drop of drool instantly fall from Uli's now hypnotized body.

When the skull spoke its ancient dialect, so did Uli, the words shooting out of her a mile a minute, morphing from the ancient tongue to what is the common tongue of Thira.

Ted was not one for violence, but a snapping out of it was in order, he shoved another saliva loaded finger in her ear, with enough disgusting syrupy wetness to break her out of whatever was happening.

"Eeeeeeeeeew! Again with the wet Willy? What's wrong with you!" Uli said, grabbing her ear, She retaliated by goosing Ted right between the legs with a back handed whip slap. Ted curled up in testicular pain.

"Why always the nuts!? Come on!" Ted howled, "What happened with the whole speaking in tongues thingy?" he asked.

"I don't know, that rotted up shit head took a hot piss in my brain or something."

"I am no rotted up piece of excrement young lady. I simply took the liberty to learn your primitive language." Oman said.

"Did it have to hurt so much?"

The skull didn't answer for a beat, until…

"No."

"Begin my reunion ceremony at once!"

"Screw that! I'm not touching it" Ted said.

"I am no IT you ill educated giant! I am Oman Zurr! One of the three scholars of the tomb of Zabok, progenitor of necromancy and you shall show me some respect."

Oman abruptly shut up, his glowing eyes darting from one side to the other. "Drat, a crack of thunder was supposed to be heard all around when my name is said, something is wrong."

"Well we are several hundred feet underground, maybe we

just can't hear it," Ted mentioned.

"Hmm yes, that's probably what happened, now gather my body you slaves and commence the reunion ceremony post haste!"

"Easy with calling people slaves Mr. Oman, the practice as well as the word was kind of banned some time ago," Uli said, respectfully of course. Oman got a good look at his two saviors wondering a good many things. One being their strange garments, from the horrid fashion he gathered it's been a long while since he croaked.

Also, they lacked any sigil of any house, second red flag. And lastly, any Necromancer with a familiar as pathetic as the one Uli had perched on her shoulder was a sure sign of a low level amateur.

"Who has awakened me from my slumber?"

Uli coughed a few and stood as straight as her minor scoliosis permitted, "Twas me milord Oman Zurr, I was told to find you by the witch known as Ogun."

"You clearly are not scholars of the Zabok! Nor descendants of my apprentices, I repeat! Why have you awakened me!?"

"My aunt told me you could help me revive the chosen one known as Prince Aiden, as well as teach me the ways of Necromancy." She added that last part, wouldn't hurt to get tutelage from one of the founding fathers of death magic.

"Prince who? And why in the name of all that is unholy would I teach you the ways of the death shepherd?"

Uli was about to give him the rundown before the room rumbled and shook, "You fools! You've led them right to me!"

"Who now?" Asked Uli.

The room shook, reacting to an unwanted presence, Uli and Ted felt the hostile pressure behind them. Two sets of eyes glowing emerald in the flickering fire lights. Their threatening presence lessened a bit by them hitting their heads on the low ceilings.

"Oh fuck me," Ted whimpered.

"Where is my auntie you green faced dildos!" Uli screamed.

The green dildos said nothing, opting to look as spooky and threatening as possible.

The dragonsack twins who have been coined as Gunther and Olaff focused their magic scanning sights on the party.

A very faint black shadow came from Uli, Blood Fucker gave off a similar hue, Ted not so much, nothing in fact, no magical aura, but Dammerung which was still slung on Ted's back shined like a road flare.

Olaff (the short one) and Gunther (the less vertically challenged one) zeroed in on Oman, he gave off an aura of purple mist. Their magic starved eyes dilated in delight as they screeched a celebratory scream, adding to the already terrifying constant rumble the room couldn't seem to shake off.

Uli and Ted covered their ears. Oman gasped at the sound, the glow in his eyes turned to a sickly yellow.

"It cannot be! Drakenstatz? Get me out of here now!"

No time for thinking, Uli grasped Oman's head.

"Those sick bastards really did it! Quick! Get my bones, we can assemble me somewhere else."

The dragonsack boys went to all fours, feline in their slow approach.

The core problem here was simple, the draconic assailants

were covering the only exit from the catacomb. They released their signature series of fire blasts out their disgusting gullets. Uli ducked and found a series of ceremonial jars, she had no idea Oman Zurr's petrified entrails filled every one, but she launched them with a pitcher's precision.

Ted hugged the wall trying to make his way to the staircase while the two evil mooks circled away from the exit. Uli was still in "throw everything you find" mode unwittingly chucking Oman's right arm and leg at the fo-dragons, "Those are my body parts, you dense bitch dog!"

"Quiet or I'll throw you too just to buy us some time," Oman saw a flash of deep purple in Uli's eyes, half pleasing him, and half actually scaring him enough to think she would launch him as a decoy.

Gunther caught one of the bones, it glowed once in contact with its slimy skin, necromantic miasma burst out of the limb, vacuumed into Gunther's mouth like taking a hit of some potent narcotic. From the looks of it necrotic magic was upsetting his stomach.

A heavy belch of black smoke, followed by a blast of black fire flew right at them.

Olaff followed up with two high pressure streams of his focused plasma shot leaving deep blackened marks on the catacomb walls.

The stop, drop and roll skills ingrained into them since preschool kicked in, both managing to dodge the barrage of magically recycled dragon breath.

They needed to get back on their feet and let themselves out in the most prompt of manners. Uli got up fine despite cradling a talking head with one arm. When Ted tried to do the same he collapsed to the floor screaming in pain.

"Get up dude come on!" Uli said.

Ted screamed as she helped him up, he could not verbalize a single coherent word. She got him up and stable and noticed two things, the smell of burnt meat, and Ted's severed right arm lifeless at their feet. Uli went white (well, whiter) with horror and joined in on Ted's mad wailing. That was enough horror to handle at the moment, but then they saw the two monstrosities position themselves for another fiery attack. Uli pulled up Blood Fucker, grabbing him like a hand gun ready to squeeze his acid bile on the foes before them, "Sorry baby," Uli said apologetically to her familiar.

"What the heck is going on here? You all know the amount of property violations you've racked up?"

All eyes now on Carl Weatherson. Uli dropped Blood Fucker, the little one relived to not be squeezed like a stress toy. Ted was momentarily relieved to see a man in law enforcement show up, till he got a good look at the cheap badge on Carl's chest stating his allegiance to the "Luminous Lakes Mall Security."

Gunther and Olaff reset their dragon breath and prepared to fire on Carl. Training and faith cut through the moment of doubt, Carl Weatherson MALL COP had a job to do!

"By the light of Etheria I condemn you!"

Uli sensing an escape about to take place was nice enough to pick up Ted's severed arm.

Carl whipped out the pendant and pointed it at the perpetrators.

Blinding white light shot out from the relic illuminating the whole room. Oman's eyes were swallowed by the light as he let out, "The Eye of Etheria!?"

A hair sized crack appeared on the pendant. Olaff and Gunther roared, their eyes burning as if hot pokers were driven through them. Carl hid the surprise of witnessing his very first miracle, a single quiet "wow," left his mouth, but enough of that, duty calls.

"Mam, Sir, I suggest we vacate the premises before those things can see again."

"We can't see either dude!" yelled Ted.

"Oh right" Carl grabbed their arms and guided them to the staircase.

While under Uli's arm, Oman looked back at the dwelling he called his temporary resting place, all his limbs left behind, now pondering his own fate as a piece of eccentric furniture.

"By the way, you two are under arrest for grave robbing."

"How about you write us up if we are actually alive in the next five minutes!" Uli said, gaining her sight back, glanced down at his plastic name tag "Carl!"

A blast fire let them know they were not out of the woods yet.

"I agree!" Carl said.

The million step staircase stood before them, the rising earthquake collapsing the stone statues into the way was a perilous touch to the situation.

"Why is the place collapsing?" huffed Ted.

"You have taken only a part of me out, a fail safe was made in case of grave robbers, you tripped it, I shall have you all made flat!"

They ran to the best of their abilities, which was not a lot, Ted's weight as well as Dammerung and Uli's platform boots caused a natural slowing to the escape, not mention Ted's on the move trauma of losing and arm. The only ones making short work of the climb was mall cop Carl and Blood Fucker scattering up the steps with rodent rapidness.

The long rows of decorative flames spilled onto the steps, adding to the shit gauntlet they were already a part of.

Olaff and his twin galloped behind them. Their eyes flaring up in the maddened ecstasy of the kill, Kalammet also getting a front row seat to the whole endeavor via their shared sight.

Carl tried to flash them again with the amulet, but no holy light showed up.

"My goddess! Have I sinned in thine eyes dear Etheria? I shall repent!"

Carl stops and drops to his knees in pious devotion.

"What are you doing dude?"

"I must repent."

"For what?!"

Carl didn't rightly know why either, his faith taught him not to ask too many questions. Ted saw both dragonsack men take aim at Uli and Carl, their magical flames let loose with nothing to shield or stop their targets from instant incineration.

That's when Ted passed out.

Carl and Uli raised their arms shielding their faces from death by solar flare.

But Instead of burning alive, Uli felt something like a stone tentacle wrap around her waist, Carl felt a shoulder ram into his torso lifting him clean off his knees.

B.F. felt getting kicked up and bit into gentle enough as to not crunch his ribs. They opened their eyes, finding themselves all on Ted, now running fast enough for a speeding ticket.

Eyes shining lightning white, muscles bulging, his entirety enveloped in an icy blue energy. His face stone cold and stoic as if deep in thought, Ted had become a magical freight train shooting its way up the staircase as if weighing nothing more than a feather.

The dragon men couldn't catch up.

Uli looked at her clumsy red headed dork, and could not believe it was him. The word that came to mind was one she would have never associated with the puppy pushover that is Ted, he looked BAD ASS, And by bad ass I mean, "I would like to climb that tree and chop it down with my hips bad ass." Uli blushed flamingo pink, sweat covering her whole body. Her senses hijacked with a heavy instinctual need to rip and tear the clothes off both Ted and herself, even with the present audience, she didn't care.

Locked under Ted's arm, with what little she could wiggle out she stretched out to fish for a kiss, the desperate attempt for lip locking went on all the way to the end of the staircase. but to the surprise of everyone not entranced by some magical guardian spirit, no exit hole was present at the end of the staircase, only a giant slab of stone.

Uli saw that the way out was no more, Ted unfazed sped up. Her desire for conky congress with Ted faded fast when she looked back and saw Gunther and Olaff catching up. The fire from the jelly filled side canals sucked up by the monsters.

Carl, calm with zen laced defeat, traced a circle and line on himself depicting the symbol of faith in the church of Etheria. "I am prepared for death. Are you?"

Uli did not register Carl's last pious statement, the mall cop felt bitter having wasted a very cool line in front of an uncaring audience moments before his demise.

Uli saw the rock slab covering the exit getting bigger, Ted was now at terminal brain splattering velocity.

"Ted, Teddy! No door up ahead dude! Whatever you're tripping on you gotta snap out of it!" but Ted chugged ahead. Carl prayed, Oman Zurr cursed and Uli said "No!" sixty five times in three seconds. They closed their eyes and braced for impact.

Olaff and Gunther wound up their respective oral flame blasts, the entire staircase went pitch black. They retched out a deafening whistle before they released their super charged attack. Everyone that wasn't a dragon or in a barbarian berserker trance screamed as if riding an exploding roller coaster.

Ted smashed into the wall face first, blood jetting out both his nostrils upon impact, splashing on the stone walls, the slab of volcanic rock exploded, Blood Fucker who was still in Ted's mouth did not appreciate the front row view of the collision .

Dust and debris from the impact clogged everyone's field of vision, Uli saw the way in or out of the tomb resealed by a buildings worth of cracked stone and cement, they made it out! She felt a dozen cuts and bruises, a couple of ribs on the verge of snapping, and her lower lip bled from biting it so hard from her recent need to bed Ted like a baboon in mating season. She took it all in a positive angle, if she could feel all that discomfort it could only mean they were still alive.

She rolled out of Ted's limp grip. "Ted! holiest of shits dude! That was amazing! How did you do that!?"

Ted wasn't moving. Gone was his blue glow, his iron muscles now spongy pillows.

Ted's sliced arm in Uli's grip flailing about during her moment of panic, "Oh no, he's dead! Don't worry bro I'll bring ya back!" she reached into her satchel for her spell book "Wait!" grunted Carl as he crawled out of the loose gravel, he turned Ted over to see the big man drooling, followed by a delicate snore with a light whistle finish to each breath due to his recently achieved broken nose. Uli's adrenaline drenched body relaxed.

"Would you apes get me out of here now?" Oman said from under a pile of drywall. Uli scuttled over and dusted the old cranium up.

"Oman, you good?" Uli asked, "It is Oman Zurr You wretched mule!"

"That's what I said, are you good though?"

"NO! I am most certainly not! What's left of my body has been reburied, and what's left of me up here has to suffer the company of touched backwater plebeians," Oman said to himself.

"You're welcome, you ungrateful jerk!" Uli said with piercing discord.

"Ungrateful? Wench! I was perfectly in bliss in my self imposed slumber, and you lot had to come around and lure a couple of drakenstatz's to feed upon my remains."

"Drakenstatz?" Uli asked, pronouncing it surprisingly well out of simple imitation.

"We call them dragonsacks."

"That's a horrible name!"

Uli and Oman felt a chill. She turned to see Carl pointing his pendant at them.

"Look Carl, Relax." Uli said as she got back on her feet.

"Necromancy! Heretics! Desecrators! Begone foul creatures!" exclaimed the mall cop, with the holy arrogance of a crusading paladin.

Oman had dealt with his fair share of acolytes in his times, "A follower of Etheria, a skittish bunch. They were marvelous sacrifices, they just loved snuffing out their own flame as long as you told them it's in the name of their sun goddess."

"Oh stop it, you're hurting the poor guy's feelings," Uli said. Having herself parents who are religious in the ways of *Ohambra*. She had learned how to dance around people of *ye way too much faith.*

Carl went for his walkie talkie "I don't know who to contact first, the police or the church, both will want their pound of flesh from you two!"

"Cool it Carl, we are not the baddies."

"I just saw you commit grave robbery and I'm guessing probably you brought that thing with demonic markings to life!"

"Demonic markings!? I beg your pardon!"

"You are covered in markings though," Uli said.

"I am? Show me!" Uli popped a compact mirror out and showed Oman the etchings. "Ah yes, yes, demonic markings sure," Oman babbled.

They were actually the phrase "small pee pee Oman" written on him by his apprentice known as Deekins using some ancient alphabet. Deekins hated Oman, and the feeling was mutual.

"Get back you feeble slave of Etheria!" Oman commanded, "Let us go or I shall cast a spell turning you into my sex pet!" Carl's mind was swallowed by the imagery suggested. Uli hoped Oman was bluffing, but still wondered how the mechanics of that would work given Oman's beheaded state.

"You are going to jail Sir! Or the church, or um, church jail!" Uli knelt next to Carl, their faces only inches apart, Carl quivered, this was the first time since his wife left him that a woman was this close to his face. The repressed past moments of his marriage combined with his personal space being invaded made Carl feel, of all things, a bit pathetic.

"We are truly sorry for being in your mall, we did not trespass, we simply never left. And the grave robbing part, well that's just not true. Grave robbing implies stealing from the dead, do you see anything dead here?" Carl turned to look at the sleeping Ted, Blood Fucker and Oman. The squirrel looked like it was dragged behind a dump truck through razor wire, any thinking person would see through the bogus semantics at hand in Uli's cross examination but something was off with Carl.

"Plus the tomb itself has been stuck in the earth for over like a million years, this is no longer considered a simple grave site, it is an archaeological site. Therefore anybody who finds it first has the right to claim it, So, I claim it"

Oman was impressed with Uli's ability to manipulate, she was clearly spewing projectiles of pure bullshit. But in his experience, it's always a good sign of a "Wizard's mind" and as you and I know, creativity is a key ingredient in the makings of magic.

Uli gave Carl the short version on what brought them there in the first place. She quickly and eloquently explained their quest of planetary salvation, and how desperately they needed extra help.

Oman saw something spark inside Carl.

A single microscopic dot began to flicker into light, a technicolor pulse made the little dot grow with every heartbeat.

Uli's magical emanations connected with Carl, as if his very soul grew hundreds of ears, paying one thousand percent attention to every syllable coming out of Uli's mouth.

A small, long dead thought was growing within Carl Weatherson, yanking itself out of the psychic graveyard it once laid silent in for years within his faith overrun mind.

Oman's gaping skull glowed with attentive interest. In one of the dozen dead languages Oman knew, he said the equivalent of, "Well I'll be dipped in shit and rolled in breadcrumbs, she brought a dead dream back to life."

"Carl, we need your help, you're our only hope my guy," his lonely mall cop eyes sparkled. The dead dream in him burst back to life. "This is it!" was on repeat in full volume within him. His resolve solidified in an instant and just like that, our merry band of misfits now had a PALADIN on a holy crusade, in Carl the Mall cop.

The roar of the recently damaged Olaff and Gunther caught Uli and Carl's attention.

"Right," Carl said with the gruffness of a seasoned soldier. He spotted a turned over shopping cart poking out of one of the half opened service closets, a sly smirk decorated his five o'clock shadow.

21

"Mr. Sundae"

Uli and company had made it out before the police descended on the Luminous Lakes Mall. The police got there forty five minutes late mind you. Busy night for Thira's finest, it was the middle of the night and most of the precinct had had one too many cold ones at detective Leonard's retirement party.

The long line of law enforcement vehicles made their way to the crime scene, yet the one at the very end slowed down to a halt. The driver looked on and saw the rest of the flashing lights get further and further away.

A tanned, nearing red face poked out of the driver's window, bleach blond hair carelessly poking out of his police hat. A half smoked cigarette clung to the corner of his permagrin smile. With the urgency of a sloth he looked around the barely lit roads devoid of any traffic or eye witnesses.

He took a deep hit and blew out a plume of smoke from his nostrils, thick and heavy in its ascending dance, far too much to come from a single drag. The wind caught it and whipped it away. The "Officer" closed his eyes, took another toke and hummed to the tune on the radio, some disco music, "the naughty stuff," he liked to call it.

His attention was brought towards the night sky, the smoke he blew out slowly returned and slithered its way back into his nose. His eyes went pale, like steam fogging up a window. His smile stretched to cheshire levels of strange.

He turned the police car on and drove straight into the visibility killing tall grass, but the cop didn't seem to mind, continuing to hum to himself in jolly tranquility.

In the middle of battling his lighter to spark up his next cigarette, he hit what felt like two speed bumps made out of fried chicken bones. "Oopsie doozle," he put it in reverse and went over the jiggly, crunchy speed bumps once more.

The mystery cop got out of his car with the cool, lazy swagger of a cowboy turned stripper movie star. "Howdy fellas, how's hunting season going?"

Gunther and Olaf looked up at the man that turned them into roadkill. Olaff's tire marked head had popped his right eye out, Gunther looked up and gave an angered screech, till he saw who it was, and decided to end his defiant cry by means of a pathetic whimper.

The cowboy cop crouched next to them, "Boss man Kalammet isn't very pleased with you two," Gunther averted his gaze as would a scolded dog, droopy eyes and all, "Let's see what you two trouble makers were up to."

He grabbed a pink filtered cigarette from his custom steel pack and lit it up, its embers sparking like cheap fireworks. He blew out the smoke into the two downed drakenstatz. They coughed to resist its entry but the smoke, sentient in its will to push in, shoved its way through every hole Gunther and

Olaff had in their crushed up faces. Like water hitting a lit fireplace, a boiling hiss echoed out of them, whatever limbs still working flayed around in agony. The "Police Officer" saw the pain being exhibited as down right boring, opting to get a good look at the multiple moons of Thira lighting up the field with fluorescent high definition. The flailing stopped with the arms and tails dropping with a wet plop. The smoke came out of them and found its way back into the officer's mouth and nostrils, bringing with it images congesting his mind's eye.

"Me oh my," he said with a twang bordering on offensive imitation, "Well that new ain't it? Or very old would be more precise."

He snuffed out the magic cigarette, grabbed both almost carcasses and dragged them to the back of the car. He popped the trunk open, and with one hand threw both recently crunched mutants inside. The naked body of Officer Philtics was already taking up most of the space, The chain smoking cop managed to close the trunk by slamming it on the stuffed bunch till the latch went click.

Gunther and Olaff let out whimpers that would have been confused with the soggy sounds of a sad long fart.

"Quiet down kids, your lucky old uncle Mr. Sundae found ya before the boys in blue did," He sat on the trunk and pressed his communicator.

"Just picked the boys up from their play date, looks like they had a bit too much fun and ran out of juice."

"It went dark when they ran through the staircase, did they retrieve it?" asked the static filled voice of Kalammet.

"That is a negatory, some red headed goon and a girl in a

witch costume have it."

"Please, your colloquialisms give me headaches, speak plainly," Kalammet said.

"The two kids still have it, there you have it, plain as a bread sandwich." Said Mr. Sundae.

A pause long enough to become awkward followed, it wasn't until the grass let up to a rural side road that Mr. Sundae let out a "Boss?" to see if the warlock was still on the line.

"Dispose of the broken drakenstaz and retrieve the blade, we will see how to get rid of it once we have it."

"Have you told tall, dark and handsome that Dammerung's back in town and all?"

Kalammet said nothing. Mr. Sundae let out a smoke infused snort, "Roger that."

"Blasted demigods, useless!" Kalammet said before taking his finger off the communicator button.

Mr. Sundae smirked, finished his smoke and used the last bits of ember to light a red filtered cigarette "Kind of expected that, but can't help myself I reckon," crimson clouds of the magical cigarette floated about with his first puff. he banged on the trunk to get the attention of the wounded creatures.

"Good news boys, you've been granted early retirement," the red smoke streams magically solidifying into scarlet spears as long as a man and as sharp as razor blades.

Mr. Sundae laughed, Olaff and Gunther cried. the hovering spears shot around Mr. Sundae into the trunk impaling the beasts. once their wailing stopped the spears lost their form, turning back to smoke fading away in the night breeze.

22

"The Weatherson Stronghold"

The house was a monument to wood paneling and thick carpet. The grandmother's house aesthetic was cozy to say the least. Mrs. Weatherson on the other hand was the antithesis of the very home she kept in tip top shape. Armored in comfortable sweats hung from her elderly thin build, years of hard housekeeping had done its worst on the woman, yet she had a stately near regal way of moving about.

"So let me get this straight, you're having a last minute get together in the garage? With your old High School buddies?"

She looked at Uli, believing her son's words just as much as she believed unicorns fall out of her hindquarters. She knew her little Carl was never the popular one.

It was late, and was willing to turn a blind eye to the fact that her son brought home a floozy. Her friend group of gossipy old folks feared Carl would one day dabble in the dark arts, and my dark arts, they meant the sinful joining of two souls in unholy congress, but if her wonderful boy was willing to sin without protection, she might get her chance to get a grandchild before her mortal coil unwinds.

"Keep it down, and don't get into the neighbor's pool, please and thank you," Mom said with the amazing fusion of motherly acceptance and tired military drill sergeant.

Carl and Uli returned to the car, both surprised that it took so little to convince the Queen Mother of the Weatherson house to oblige to the impromptu co-ed sleepover.

Ted laid out in the back of the car, with the giant sword as his bedfellow. His hazy brain could only focus on the skull of Oman and Blood Fucker, who for the whole ride home were having a staring contest, to Ted's money the skull was going to be victorious, he had the no eyelid advantage.

Blood loss and losing an appendage had left his mind a bit more simpler than usual.

They drove the station wagon into the two car garage that served more as a storage facility.

They plopped Ted out on a sleeping bag and dragged him over to what Carl called his man cave. The old couch and mismatching lawn chairs on top of the century old rug really did tie the room together.

"Thank you Carlos," Ted said.

"You're welcome, and it's Carl."

"Oh really!? Where is he at?" Carl pondered clarifying but realized It would fall to deaf ears at the moment.

"Carlos I'm sorry, you've been so nice to us despite imploding your place of work." Ted said.

Carl had long left Ted's side, he was behind the car taking a good look at Dammerung, a blade still spoken about within his dying faith. Though erased from most history and local faiths, the older religions still had tales of the dimensional blade's existence, though in Carl's dogma, it was the blade of the Goddess Etheria, which she would use to smite the evils of the world.

He knew, something just told him. Something divine, a symbol of his faith was just laying in the back of a station wagon, this has to be providence for sure, a clear sign of his revived purpose as a Paladin for Etheria.

Oman, feeling a bit ignored on the coffee table, decided to speak up.

"If we are going to reattach the arm to that brute of yours, we must do it as soon as possible, we delay any longer and the ritual could produce, shall we say, less than favorable results."

"Less than favorable results?" Ted asked, voice shaking like somebody added a digital effect to it. Oman opted to jump the question section of the presentation all together.

"Quick, retrieve the arm apprentice," Uli went for the arm still in the station wagon, wrapped in even more dirty clothes. Blood Fucker was nibbling on the little finger. "B.F. No! Bad Familiar! Bad!" Uli barked, half meaning it, half not wanting to hurt her cute little demon's feelings. Then, Oman's words finally hit her.

"Wait, did you just call me apprentice?!"

"It seems I am currently stuck with you and your team of halfwits. Assisting you in your quest as well as educating such raw material as yourself may serve me in the future," Oman said.

"A future where you do nefarious super evil stuff?" Uli asked.

"Perhaps, what say you? Apprentice."

"Deal," Uli answered.

"Bit quick to make a deal with a skull who basically confessed to doing evil if given the chance," Carl said.

"Oh come on dude, it's a skull, the most evil thing he can do at the moment is bite your toes."

Carl gave Oman a weary look to which Oman answered by snapping his jaw twice with gleeful malice.

"I've got my eyes on you, skull!" Carl said with the authoritative tone of a law man.

"Do as you wish, slave of Etheria, it matters not to me. Now then, the arm if you please apprentice," Uli placed the arm before her new teacher, the joy of being called apprentice still ringing in her ears.

Oman focused on the limb, he darted his glowing eyes to Uli. "Time is dwindling, turn me to the poorly dressed Paladin" Uli did so, "Now! Acolyte of light, I need the following to make this man whole again."

"You're going to perform a ritual here? On my property?!" his mother's property but anyways.

"I am not sure how to feel about this," Carl looked at Uli with his honest brown eyes, "Look I want to help, both my job and faith say so, but, necromancy? In my family home? That leaves a dark mark on the place you know, cursed soil where it was practiced and all that."

Uli didn't have two hours to give her "necromancy is not dark magic" manifesto.

"Carl please, Ted needs our help, the whole curse nonsense was only made up to discourage everyone and their dog from doing back room necromantic surgery. Do you have any idea how many medical professionals would be on the street if this was still available?" Uli said.

My apprentice speaks the truth," Oman said, doing his best effort to make his beyond the grave, reverb heavy voice sound more amicable.

Carl didn't pay attention to Oman, mostly because he was pondering the present moral dilemma, and he had a natural aversion to reanimated skulls.

"Fine!" Carl said, slapping his thighs and looking at the sealing, "Etheria help me, what do you need skull man?"

"Blessed oil and string doused in the ashes of sacrificed animals."

Carl expected far worse, he inhaled slowly "I can do this," he walked out in a hurried purposeful stride, he may not like the things he has to do sometimes, but Carl didn't half ass anything in his life, even playing goon to a skull about to perform dark magic in his garage.

He also needed a bit of time away from the cyclone of chaos he had been sucked into for the past two hours.

As the overwhelmed saintly security guard left the garage, Oman Zurr's teeth chittered with joy. The skull hadn't been able to engage in arcane tomfoolery in a while, he was jazzed about getting to be magically naughty. Even if he was playing mere second banana assistant to the dim Necromancer in training that is Uli.

Uli cleared some space just a few feet away from the orange soda stained rug and helped Ted over and to lay down on the cold polished cement floor.

"This is gonna hurt like a bitch isn't it?" Ted asked, fear translated through the tremble in his voice, his hand curled up in a white knuckle clutch.

"Straight talk, no clue, but I promise you that with every inch of my existence I will try to make this as painless as possible."

"Splendid, Uli, would you please lightly stab him and use his blood to make a circle," Oman said, as if kicking off the start of his own arcane cooking show.

"Excuse me, my blood?"

"Like only a little right?" Uli asked.

"You want to save his limb and dabble in your affinity don't you? Now buck up and prepare to summon the gears of creation and destruction to your will. This is your first lesson Uli Einsworth, and so far you're failing."

23

"Devil is in the Detail"

Renegade? Yes.
Rebel, misfit? Always.
But failing? Never! Uli may be a lot of things, but a slacker academically was never one of them. Straight "A" student since preschool and damn proud of it. Oman could sense it and knew that any notion of the word *"failing"* was going to ruffle a feather or two, wizards know the weight of words, even when not used for incantations, at times a simple word can cause a more volatile reaction than a fully realized spell, and Oman liked the power in that.

Uli produced her dagger from her bag, found some rubbing alcohol in Carl's prominently displayed first aid box, she disinfected it and rubbed some of the alcohol on Ted's shoulder.

"Close your eyes, It'll only be a small prick."

"Like how small are we talking about?" Ted asked. Uli opted for the surprise attack and pricked him deep enough to get a small controlled drip of blood.

Ted screamed a few octaves higher than usual and couldn't

help but give Uli a reprimanding slap on the hand.

"What is wrong with you! Seriously? Sneak attack?" Uli bit her lip and grimaced, dirty pool yes, but it must be done.

She finger painted a circle around Ted, many spells and rituals use blood in their practices, but none put so much importance to it as the Necromancers do, paradoxically, the very fuel of life is required when dealing with the occult matters of the dead.

She grabbed the detached arm, which was heavier than most people think a dead limb weighs.

She dropped the floppy appendage on its fingers first on the hard floor, a couple of snaps let the garage dwellers know to add broken fingers to the injury list Ted had piled up that night.

"Oh shit, sorry, so sorry!" Uli said. Ted was grateful that he was not attached to his arm.

"Place the arm next to the stump now," Oman commanded, "Mark the arm with the following words," He recited the incantation, but to the common modern ear it sounded like baby gibberish spoken through a serial killer's voice modulator.

"Yeah, I don't know how to write that."

"Blast it woman, just write what you think it sounds like, and repeat it on the stump as well!"

She got a permanent marker out and scribbled on Ted what she could best interpret phonetically was the incantation, *Glied verloren, Glied gefunden.*

"How is this supposed to work?" Uli asked, "Ted's not dead, do we have to kill him first?"

Ted lifted his head, eyes flashing fury at his friend. Uli

turned and worded out "kidding" and patted his shoulder.

"Yes, this would be far easier if he lacked breath, but one works with what they have, but I like where your head's at," said the skull, with sadly no pun behind that golden opportunity.

"What?" Uli asked.

"Hush now child!"

"Don't hush me!" Uli responded.

"Silence! Do not let your tiny brain be stuck in the old ways, I have seen in you what my archaic brethren failed to grasp of necromancy, it is not just about manipulating dead humans and beasts. Death! ALL things live and die, every single piece of matter taking space has a life cycle, even the very gods themselves expire in one way or another," Oman continued his rant, "All that lived must perish, when it does it leaves something behind, an echo, a register of its once essence, If it is not utilised and returned to the prime source ley lines as to keep the flow going, the whole magical ecosystem halts. That is where Necromancers come into play, we retrieve it, recycle it, and return it to the flow of magic."

"So we are magic hippie trash men for dead stuff? Vultures with witch hats?" Uli asked.

"That is offensive to the Necroman… no, that actually is an appropriate analogy," Oman said, enjoying the spooky yet whimsical imagery it promotes.

Carl returned with the things, as well as a plate of cookies, baby carrots and milk, Mama Weatherson was just happy her thirty-something little boy had real life, not made up or living in another continent, actual friends. Though the snack option made it clear that to her mama hen eyes, Carl just turned twelve yesterday.

"Okay I got the stuff, but I had to improvise and substitute some of them, didn't have dead animal ashes, but we did have some cigarette ash I mixed up with the remains inside the mosquito zapper, I dunked some of my moms yarn in it, and all I had was cooking oil so I said a prayer to it thats should do right?"

Oman again missed his arms, one hand would suffice to slap Carl for his lack of respect for the craft and its ingredients.

The skull sighed and eyed the things as they were placed before him, "In the end it is more about the importance you put on the tools you use, but subpar ingredients may produce subpar dishes." Oman long ago wanted to be a chef in his youth, but after burning a chicken coop's worth of fowl and eggs made him take up his second elective. But he still loved the fact that cooking and death magic were almost the same in many principals.

"Tie each end of the string to the stump and arm, then douse both of them in oil," Uli obeyed promptly.

"For this to work we need Theodore."

"It's Ted." Ted said.

"I don't care, Theodore and Uli must..."

"Why did you get her name right?" Ted interrupted.

"Hush you brainless buffoon!" Oman said, very much done with Ted's general existence.

"Both of you require an anchor, think of it as the main ingredient that you will put the condiments and herbs on," Oman continued,"The barbarian will use a strong memory connected to the severed appendage, all things have memories connected to them, memories hold power, the stronger the memory, the stronger the spell it can manifest. Uli will do the same."

"A strong memory about his arm?"

"No! Did the collective intelligence of humanity plummet to the many hells in the last millennia? Your job isn't just to spew out gibberish and wave your hands around like a drunken monk. Necromancy deals with the dead, but also…"

Uli's ears twitched like a rabbit finding a carrot, "Life!"

"Congratulations, the I.Q. of the entirety of Thira rose by one point just now. Theodore, now think of your arm, Uli! Say the words and anchor it with creation, will it to be true!"

Uli chanted the words she jotted down on Ted as she delved into her mind, searching her memory bank. She thought about the moment she was at aunt Ogun's place and saw Harriet (auntie's long time dog,) had a litter of pups, the thought of such a good dog making more of her was proof that life didn't suck all the time.

The crusted old blood around Ted's pieces glowed with a black hued light. Carl smiled, though little the time spent with Uli, he felt a warmth seeing the little goth go getter tap into not only her talent, but something she loves.

"Sustain that thought!" Oman yelled over the hum of the magic happening around them. His eyes shot over to Ted, "Theodore, she built the bridge, you have to meet her half way, find the good memory of your arm now!"

"How am I supposed to have a good memory of an arm?!" Ted pondered.

Uli screamed in agony, sparks popping within the blue flame, threatening to cause harm.

"OW! What the hells?" Uli yelped.

"You fool! Your mind fuels the power! Your negative thoughts are corrupting the spell, you're hurting your friend, now do it, a good memory! Now!"

"I don't know what you want from me?" Ted yelled. Uli's next scream came with a good helping of blood.

"Ted! Please work with me here!" Uli said.

"Now Theodore!" said Oman. Ted's arm twitched to life, thrashing about like a fish out of water. The arm lost what little color it had left in it, a necrotic gray staining it whole.

"You're losing all connection to your arm, leaving it perfect for possession. If you don't start thinking happy thoughts about your fucking arm, you're going to kill Uli and anything else with a pulse within a city block. Do you understand!?"

Ted looked over at his friend who was doing everything she could to save his arm.

In the violent chaos, a tattered old poster caught his attention, some big haired and even bigger chested woman was promoting a national hot dog franchise, though not per say lewd, even an innocent simpleton could figure out what they were trying to allude to in the promotional material.

This is where Ted finally found his happy thought.

The arm stopped convulsing, the blood and permanent marker runes glowed a stable dark blue. Before anybody could relax, Uli saw Carl gesturing some holy symbol from his chest to his face, eyes closed shut. She turned to look at Ted and found the arm pumping away to an invisible rod like a teen who just figured out what a certain appendage was for.

"Oh Teddy, really?" Uli said, more humor than disappointment in her tone. "What?!" he said defiantly, "Like you could come up with happier moments involving an arm."

"Playing catch with your Dad, drawing your first rainbow,

saving a bug and taking it outside, punching a bully," Ted wanted to refute, but as forever, Uli was right, and he's a pervert apparently.

"Now focus on binding the two thoughts, this is the catalyst!" Oman said with a glee he thought his nonexistent heart couldn't muster up anymore.

"Imagine a waterfall running through your arms," Uli was doing pretty good, but

Carl's Holy Sigil flared up, aggravated by the taboo ritual happening before it. It's light so hot it burned through Carl's favorite uniform.

The arm flapped around wildly, Uli kept an eye open to keep watch on the hellish horny appendage.

"Get the eye of Etheria out of here!" Carl went outside, looking in from the dirt covered window on the door.

"Focus girl!" Oman pressed.

"Pump master 5000 is making too much noise!" the fluorescent lights in the garage flickered and dimmed.

"You are losing claim to the magic used! Something else is trying to take the arm!"

A heavy aura warped gravity so hard and so fast, the stomach of every person in the garage felt slammed out of their bodies.

"Complete the chant child! A dark one is reaching for the arm!"

"But if I complete the incantation without binding it's gonna be a faulty spell!"

"Better that than a demonic arm doing gods knows what to us all! Close the ritual!"

Uli closed her eyes, concentrated on the spell, the runes burned bright, like two magnets snapping into each other the arm fused. Ted let out a scream at the foreign feeling of your body reattaching itself, bone by bone, nerve by pain screaming nerve. Yet his voice wasn't the only one screaming, dozens of unseen mouths shrieked, all of them coming from Ted's arm.

Uli was about to finish closing the spell, when Ted's face wiped around to look straight at her. She knew the moment their eyes met, she wasn't looking at Ted, it wasn't Ted in beef cake mode, it was something else.

"One mistake, one false move and he is mine!" The voice vibrated in her head, an echo chamber bouncing on every corner of her mind, both so high pitched it could crack glass, but so baritone it could smash a house with the weight under the tone.

Uli shook like she was plunged into the arctic, her senses, her very soul locked up.

"Stupid child! Finish the spell!" yelled Oman.

The demon within Ted turned to look at Oman.

"Ah, the blasphemy is here," Oman's eyes gleamed a thin light to Ted's now occupied body.

"I shall finally bring you to the abyss for your punishment!" hunger dripping from every syllable.

"Not today, not ever you decayed devil!"

Uli used the distraction to finish the ritual, repeating one last time its sacred gibberish, a kinetic blast shaped like a ripple in water blew all present down to the ground.

No one moved. All digesting what had just transpired, threats from a demon, wonderful, just wonderful.

A scream broke the silence, a pitch just as high as the demon's. It was Uli, fists pumped and punched the air from her lying position.

"Holy shit what happened?" Ted looked down and saw his arm, fully functional and no coat of cadaver gray to it. Ted broke into tears.

"You did it, Uli! You fucking did it!" Ted rejoiced, "Oh shit, cookies!"

Carl collected the cookies and brought them to Ted, not just because he wanted a better look at the arm, but because he was a good host of course.

Blood Fucker leapt on to Ted and squeaked in celebration. Ted has now been touched not only by death, but by a demonic entity! B.F. and him were practically related at this point. Brothers serving under the same Necromancer.

Uli stopped punching at nothing and collected her thoughts. The cold concrete floor grounding her back to the reality of it all. She pulled her spell book out and furiously wrote down the new incantation in her arsenal.

"Victory? Is that what you're feeling girl?" Oman said.

"What?!" Uli snapped. "I did it, didn't I?"

"Yes! You did it! You almost botched a whole spell because a little noise distracted you!" Oman snorted out a plume of dirt stuck in his nostril, "You do have the raw components despite starting so old. But you almost let something into our world that could have been more evil than the villains you wish to thwart in your own realm. Doom Uli Einsworth, doom! Every time you summon the force arcane, always remember you're wielding a knife where the grip is just as sharp as its blade. one misstep or lack of respect to it, and it will make you bleed."

The reality in what the talking head just said was a bit too real for Uli's taste, she mentally chimed out and looked at Ted chatting it up with Carl.

The flashes of what just happened made a comeback into

her consciousness. She had never been in the presence of such oppressive malevolence, the demon's words condensed into such hatred it hurt just to listen to them. She finally got the lecture Oman was flogging her with, she's dealing with hazardous materials, handle with care.

"But," Oman said, "You did complete the spell," Uli was taken aback by the way the skull said it, it was warm, fuzzy even, but with the right sprinkle of spookiness.

Uli welled up with a feeling very alien to her, this elusive thing they call pride. She doesn't get complimented that often, much less by a peer in the ways of the unliving.

"Why did that thing call you *The Blasphemy*? Nasty insult coming from a demon," Uli asked.

Oman went quiet, eyes a small but steady within. "When this is all over ask me again, just talking about them gives them power, and I revile the idea of giving such vermin any gram of it,"

Uli didn't feel like pressing the subject, paranormal gossip can be aired out another day.

A shiver drummed to life inside her bones, cold as northern ice. She braced for impact, she knew what was coming, the one thing she never liked about the whole wizard and witch business.

"Fuck, here comes the rebound," Uli sat next to the closest wall, she put her knees to her chest and hugged them.

"This is going to hurt isn't it?" Uli asked.

"Big spells are taxing on a mortal shell, now endure, it doesn't hurt for long."

Uli braced for impact. The cold was going to get bad for a couple of minutes. She felt every part of her body bend the knee to the death magic paying its price. As she contended with what felt like an icicle from brain to buttocks. She still managed to blurt out with absolute honesty...

"Still worth it."

24

"Sort of Ranger Carl"

Carl handed out sleeping bags, Ted didn't fit into any of them so he got a huge blanket with a green tiger on it, and loved it. They filled Carl in on the sword's compass like power.

"Etheria works in mysterious ways. Maybe the chosen one prophecy is still in play, omens don't trade on exact dates, this just might be the way things happen."

"I am amazed religious zealotry is alive and well in the modern age," Oman stated, laying the condescension thick at the end.

"Oh it's also fun to see that religious intolerance hasn't changed much since your day," Carl retorted.

Uli has enough religious family to know this isn't going to end well, so she opted to change the subject.

"Any clue who is throwing these dragon boy freaks at us?"

"Make no mistake, the return of the holy blade has probably been noticed by anybody with enough magic talent." Oman said, "I don't think they've deduced your intentions, but the presence of the blade is enough to make them a little nervous."

"So we have to go low profile, no freeways or big crowds," Carl said.

"So how are we going to get there, for that matter, where is THERE anyways?" Ted asked.

Carl rubbed his five o'clock shadow. Non said it, but all felt it gave his bland complexion a bit of an old action hero look to him.

"What direction does the sword move?" Carl asked. Uli snapped her finger, "Blood Fucker, Be a good squirrel and hop on the sword for a second."

Blood Fucker skittered and hopped on to the great big sword.

Dammerung lit up instantly, its wind chime melody filled the garage, slowly levitating the grip and guard up, B.F. hung on like a pirate on a crow's nest as it floated north east till it panged against the garage door.

"Such is the power of Etheria!" Carl said, more surprised than scared at this point.

Though slow, the sword began to bend the garage door with its forward drive.

"Okay baby, Off the sword." Uli commanded.

B.F. happy to obey, the "baby" part really tickled his fancy. He hopped off on to the tarp covered car and the sword clanked to the floor. Carl was offended by how these heathens treated the holiest of holy relics. He scratched his neck as his eyes looked around for an answer. He got up and went to a stack of old cardboard boxes with lids on them.

"What are you doing?" Uli asked.

Carl didn't answer, attentively reading each sticker on the

boxes.

"When I was applying to be a Park Ranger, I thought it would give me an edge if I knew all the state parks and maps of Thira."

"Wanted to teachers pet your way up the ladder I see?" Ted scoffed.

"Won't deny the tactic, but if getting to learn new stuff is the price, then it's a pretty sweet deal."

Ted then knew Carl was probably bullied in high school.

"Aha!" Carl barked, he pulled out a large foldable map from one of the boxes.

He spread it out on the floor between the circle of sleeping bags. Oman was about to protest that he wanted to see, but Uli put him onto the map before he could complain.

It was a map detailing the greater continent that comprised Thira's largest land mass, once divided between the Forlen Empire and the joint nations of Hilliden, now all under Forlen rule. The map had multiple dots denoting the parks and untamed forest sections of the world.

He pointed to a little spot with an X, "We are here," he announced, tracing his finger from it directing it north east. "So the sword is always on the move this way..." Carl outlined a path with his finger north east, "It's on its way to Aiden's tomb, but that could be five minutes away or halfway around Thira for all we know, we could be following for years."

Carl's finger ran by a drawing that looked like a crescent moon coffee stain surrounded by little black trees.

"What is that there?" Uli asked Carl.

"Oh that is a topographical depiction of a crater, and that stuff around it is a black wood forest."

Uli's eyes bulged as she tapped the crater on the map, "It's there, it is so there," Uli said with confidence as she placed Blood Fucker on the location like a giant marker.

B.F. looked down on the map confused, he wanted to pee but opted to wait, all were looking at him and he was prone to a shy bladder.

"Alzahar Crater!" Uli shouted, "It's the place we saw in the sword video flashback spell at Ogun's, where all the stuff happened with Aiden and the horse and crap!"

"What horse stuff?" Carl asked.

"Tell ya later, but if his body was somewhere it would be there right? At the final fight in the middle of a creepy black forest"

"Oh that forest is a doozy. That particular black forest is a BLOOD BLACK FOREST, it has a creepy reputation amongst locals and Rangers alike, some say its drenched in the blood of thousands, and that evil spirits mutated the local wildlife," Carl informed the crew with his practiced but never used Park Ranger tour guide delivery.

"All the more proof that's where we need to go, something doesn't get that kind of a back story unless it has something to hide in it." Uli said.

"What if we see more of those dragon freak boys again?" Ted asked.

"They feed on magic, perhaps cursed forest energy is bad for their diet, or at the very least, throw them off if they show themselves again." Oman said.

"Look at you, contributing comments to the team, sounds like you're starting to like us," Uli said.

"Even pig farmers grow fond of their swine, it's inevitable." Oman added with disdain.

"So, blood forest, evil spirits and a possible dragon death pit?" Ted said, adding up how much he hates all of this.

Silence surrounded the council of the two car garage, they pondered the options, which was either death by magic eating dragons, or death by blood forest.

Ted looked over to Uli, "It's your hero's quest, your call."

"I don't know how much time we have, but it's probably not a lot until someone eventually finds us again. We're in too deep anywho, can't quit even if we wanted to," that last line made Ted's heart fart, but he knew it to be true as well.

Uli struck the map with her right index finger, landing next to Blood Fucker startling him enough to urinate a bit on the map.

"Blood forest it is!" announced Uli.

"For Etheria!" Exclaimed Carl.

"To destiny or death!" Oman followed.

"All of you said something cool, If I say something now it will only be compared to what he said," Ted mewled.

Blood Fucker as to join in on the revelry squeaked and flapped his vestigial wings.

And thus, the out of shape five percent Barbarian, a Necromancer's apprentice, a mall cop Paladin, a talking skull, a semi sentient sword and an undead squirrel made an unspoken pact.

The fellowship of the two car garage was made.

25

"Dinner Party"

Back at the capitol, it all looked like business as usual. Volshtadt sat at his too long dining room table as he entertained too many diplomats and high ranking officials from across all of Thira. All sworn fealty to his name and country for some time now.

Volshtadt kept his polite smile as he saw them chit up a chat while enjoying their extravagant dinner.

His attention went to the young diplomat from Voran Sammat, his dark tan and jet black hair contrasting against his emerald eyes made him an obvious hit with any gender you could mention.

The blood line was clear, some distant descendant of King Sammat the second, the striking eyes and wolfish grin made it a dead giveaway.

After the death of Aiden, King Sammat the second was the last ruler to ever defy Volshtadt's ascendance to the throne of Thira.

Chosen boy extraordinaire Aiden was the best of friends

with Sammat and his men. In the battle of Alzahar crater, the desert king led the vanguard, prideful of being the ones who cleared the way for Prince Aiden to make his way to the Evil King.

The local Faith of the desert kingdom further boosted the ferocity of the Sammatrian fighters. Death in battle meant that your soul went to an infinite orgy on the fields of *Anharat*, Goddess of life and lust. If you just died of natural causes, like old age or cirrhosis, your soul simply vanished into the night sky of the *Anharat* fields, forever forced to just watch as the heroes of the desert folk forever got their jolly's jumbled with. So everyone made a point of dying in some kind of fight. It was known that they would actually tie their elderly to drugged up horses and have them ride into battle, because the scholars of the faith of *Anharat* believed it (their words verbatim) "Still counted."

Followed by fifty thousand of his *Sarraffen* royal guardsmen, King Sammat rode to the capitol for vengeance, with a magically charged sandstorm hiding their numbers.

Volshtadt day dreamed of the sand cloaked army, their faces in mid climax at the idea of war and sex.

By that time in the new rule of Volshtadt, most of the other nations had fallen in line behind him. But not these blood hungry warriors of Voran Sammat.

Kalammet's plan for global takeover was working a bit too well, making the whole endeavor a bit boring from time to time. So the once called Voidlord welcomed some fresh violence delivered right at his doorstep.

He walked out to meet the king and his army. Volshtadt smiled as the warriors crashed upon him like waves of gold, blades and blood. Each attack from his demon dimension sword Thigg sent dozens of men flying. But if their heart still made a beat, the Sarrafen Royal Guardsmen would find a way to get up and charge again until they got their ticket to the great big love train in the sky.

When King Sammat made it to Volshtadt, eighty percent of his royal forces laid slaughtered under the boots of the king of calamity.

Sammat was royalty but mortal all the same, so he came up with a plan.

Legend says before he clashed with his ultimate foe, he made a dozen deals with demon and pagan gods alike, as to harness some of their demonic power to confront Volshtadt on common ground.

The evil entities gladly accepted Sammat's request, the higher powers that be were alarmed and confused on what happened with Volshtadt and the breaking of prophecy.

Hellions and death gods are a superstitious lot you know, prophecy unfulfilled filled them up with as much anxiety as any mortal citizen of Thira.

King Sammat arrogantly thought he double crossed a buffet of deities and was about to set the scales of time and tradition back in place. Going as far as believing he was the true chosen one. I mean, all the other ones were these arrogant pale skinned weaklings, maybe the fates felt the prophecy needed more variety to it.

Sammat crossed swords with Volshtadt, every parry and thrust destabilized reality to the point of causing earthquakes and tornadoes.

The bout, though epic in proportion, lasted only a matter

of minutes. King Sammat used his combined might of the demons and gods he bartered with, but it still wasn't enough.

Volshtadt was designed to be the zenith of pure condensed malice in the world. Chaos and darkness itself bent to his will simply by him existing. What Sammat was bringing to the bout just wasn't up to snuff.

When King Sammat fell, it wasn't just because the embodiment of destruction and doom was disintegrating him with a sword forged of a hell dimension. His body could not handle the demonic power he signed up for.

The desert king just popped off, and I mean that in the most literal way, his head shot off his body halfway out the atmosphere, while an eruption of spirits spiraled out of his body, escaping back to the worlds between worlds.

That was the last time Volshtadt savored the glorious rush of combat, the pulsing forward motion of violent purpose. Moulding the future with each slash of his sword! And in a huff and a puff, just like that, all that fun stuff was gone.

A mild applause broke him away from his flashback. Once he fell back to reality the first thing he saw was the sword of King Voran placed in front of him, perfectly exhibited in a lovely lacquered display box. It had been restored and polished to its former glory, a curved two handed sword with a patterned inlay all over the blade. The forgework was made to resemble a tornado whirling inside of its dark steel. A red jewel inlaid at the center represented the unifying of the five desert Kingdoms under the Voran banner. Volshtadt felt his life mirrored in that ornate weapon of war, displayed in a case for any mouth breather to ogle at it.

He relaxed an ounce once he saw the heir to Voran Sammat standing on the other side of the table, sipping the last drop of wine from his glass.

Later that night Volshtadt learned that the young man gave a pretty damn good speech before presenting the sword. The young man known amongst his people as Prince Ralan had a gift for public speaking.

Volshtadt stood up and raised his glass to meet the heir's. He was a descendant of his last great foe, some respect to the last remnant of King Sammat was due.

"I thank you all for coming today. your friendship and support to this brotherhood of nations has been constant and never fading, I should know, since I've been here for more time than I am willing to admit in front of such a young and vibrant group of guests." He said with his best fake-sincere voice he has practiced for a couple thousand years now. Polite and quiet chuckles bounced around the lavishly decorated dining hall.

Despite his programmed monologue, President Volshtadt could not stop from looking at Prince Ralan every chance he could get. His emerald eyes would take him back to that fire, to the blood, to the mountains made of his fallen foes.

The heir simply stared back with a smile and nodded in agreement to whatever Volshtadt spoke.

The nods and constant eye contact by Ralan, did not come off as social etiquette in Volshtadt's eyes. He understood a bit differently. Volshtadt was willfully ignorant to the fact he started this awkward stare match, but why get bogged down by such trivialities.

He was built to be a predator, and such creatures take prolonged eye contact as an invitation to confrontation in the most violent of terms, also maybe to mate, but Volshtadt lost the taste for that some time ago.

Volshtadt smiled at the idea, Ralan smiled back exactly at the moment he shouldn't have. As far as the President is concerned, the game was set and he got the first move. To his credit he processed all of these swirling emotions without skipping a beat of his post dinner speech.

"With this gift of a far ancient time, let us look at it as a milestone of progress. Gone are the barbaric tools of the past, every day more and more seen only as scraps of history to be forgotten," Volshtadt paused for dramatic effect, "To be put in a corner, allowing time to do its due diligence, till we're just thrown away."

The party got dead quiet, not knowing if they should clap, say amen, or run away. The heir to Voran Sammat smiled but his face gleamed with sweat.

Kalammet started a quick and nervous clap, "Well said! Well said!" affirming and accepting grunts and similar noises abounded for a moment.

"But..." Volshtadt said, "But certain things endure, certain things, despite the passage of time demand respect, and blood."

He made his right into a fist, he hammered the display box open and slid the Sammatrian sword on the table over to prince Ralan.

"That blade was forged with the promise of tasting my blood, I'm curious if Sammatrians still have enough of a spine to keep their promises."

Not a single soul moved. Kalammet equally paralyzed, a storm was stirring in the room, an none could escape. The old wizard knew this, and at this point, he had learned a long time ago, that once the boss got like this, best just to weather the storm till he got his fix.

The table rattled, the floors creaked and cracked. light bulbs popped and hissed to death.

"Well," Volshtadt said, "Pick it up," Ralan didn't move an inch but didn't look away either. "Pick it up, honor the king that preferred getting his soul chopped and shared to demons for eternity rather than bend the knee to me."

Ralan woke up thinking he was just going to shake a few hands, kiss an ass or two, and get a free meal while visiting the capital of everything in Thira.

Now he's being asked by the most messed up ruler in history to engage in glorious mortal combat with Ralan's success rate below the negative line. This was not why he took a twenty two hour flight with two layovers.

"Mr President, I could never raise a weapon at you, I am here simply respecting the pacts my ancestors did," Ralan said, not knowing half of the things that happened way back when, due to the globally revised history of Thira, "If I did anything to offend, I beg your pardon."

Volshtadt didn't look away, he raised his right hand and his beloved blade Thigg shot to him, perfectly falling into his grip. He slowly peeled it from the scabbard. Every ear in the room bled from the sonic attack of agonising screams and laments flooding into the room. The sword forged from a hell dimension loved to be beckoned on for more souls.

"Pick the sword up!"

"My lord, perhaps we should retire for the night?" Kalammet said, desperately keeping some decorum.

Volshtadt's incandescent eyes pierced into his advisor with torch light focus. If not for the wizard's many mental mystic barriers he would have bowed down to the psychic force the king was pumping into the whole building.

"Quiet Kalammet, or I'll ask you next if you have forgotten the good old days."

Kalammet looked away, the crash of a few plates and glasses secured the attention of Volshtadt back to Prince Ralan.

Now holding King Sammat's sword. His grip was off but functional, but what got the evil king's blood surging with joy was the look in Ralan's eyes. He saw the brazen fury, ego and gusto for gore his long dead rival once played in as well.

The heir took a stance that tried to look like he had any idea what he was doing. His brave essence swirled around him, Volshtadt could feel how the good Prince was trying to suppress his fear enough to act if necessary. But the shaking blade and the weak knees couldn't help but tattle on Ralan's all consuming terror.

Volshtadt's senses calmed. His demonic essence flying out of him like a piston relieving pressure. He let out a sigh and dropped his sword Thigg on the nicely carpeted floor. The horrific screams quieted to absolute silence.

"Brave of you Prince, I commend you for even lifting that thing up, you've done more than Aiden ever had a chance to, and for that you have my thanks," Said Volshtadt, "But sadly, whatever power and fighting spirit your family had, died a long time ago," Ouch, that stung, yet Volshtadt went on,"I apologize for tonight's behavior, it's...been an odd couple of days."

Kalammet's body relaxed from the release of pressure in the room, his mad dash to get the night back on track was derailed before he had a chance to assess his next move, he looked over Volshtadt's shoulder and all he could bring himself to say was…

"Oh fuck all."

The heir to Voran Sammat had a lapse in survival instinct caused by having his pride pissed on, he lifted the sword and charged towards Volshtadt. The old blood was perhaps gone, but for a brief second every instinct in Ralan's body commanded him to take out the President.

A very earnest attempt at a battle cry came from Ralan as he raised the sword ready to bring it down on the impossible foe before him. Volshtadt didn't even bother dodging, he let the kid take his swing. The curved sword crash landed on Volshtadt's left shoulder. Not even a single fiber on Volshtadt's coat broke. A synchronised gasp from the guests at hand announced the end of the bout.

He was at the very least mildly amused that the royal rich boy showed some backbone, but the good Prince Ralan of Voran Sammat did raise a sword against him. Sure, Volshtadt started the whole mess, but still, the rules are the rules.

"Again, brave, but…" Thigg leapt back to his owner's hand, it then flashed through Ralan's neck at lightning speed.

The prince's head slid off hitting the floor with a dull thunk. The massive pressure of presence from Volshtadt made Ralan's Blood and other important innards jet out the newly made orifice, decorating the dining hall. Panic took over the room. Volshtadt let terror run rampant for a moment, after the appropriate amount of despair, he raised his finger to his mouth and very gently went "Sh."

Silence, either by his will or by the guest's own survival

mode kicking in, either way they all shut the hell up.

"Well that was about two seconds of fun," Volshtadt said.

Kalammet walked through the newly hung viscera decorations towards his boss, "Are you happy now sir?" He said, making sure he nailed the sarcastic exhaustion to perfection. Volshtadt picked up on it, his death stare found his advisor with near cybernetic velocity. If Volshtadt's looks could kill, this particular one would be a three year war crime packed into a split second. The ancient warlock faded out of the room like a chastised ghost, off to cry to some dark corner of a haunted house.

"Again I apologize to you all for having to see that brazen act of rebellion from the heir of Voran Sammat, but you all did nothing and just sat back and watched," the hell blade Thigg roared for more souls, "And if you ask me, that's just as bad as stabbing me yourselves."

Volshtadt proceeded to brute force gravity magic. He cracked his neck twice, conjuring the weight of a dead star to fall into the room, the delegates had no time to panic, all made into flesh dinner plates. Volshtadt had genuinely smiled more times that night than he had in the last thousand years. He grabbed his wine and walked out of the dining hall feeling a bit bad for the clean up crew. He knows Roger on the janitorial staff, nice guy.

He made sure to comp the janitor's lunch for a few weeks.

* * *

Kalammet stood in the darkest corner he could find, "What are we to do with the remains my King?"

"Bag them and send them back to their homes Kalammet. I doubt it'll cause enough of a stink for them to do something, but a guy can dream can't he?"

"As you wish," The warlock did a slow reverence that dipped lower than needed.

He saw Volshtadt, his creation, walk away to do gods knows what with the rest of his night. But the dining room, looking like a vampire blood rave made it clear that something had cracked in the commander and chief.

"Dammerung's return is to blame," Kalammet told himself, the irony of a weapon of peace causing a creature made of raw magic to commit murder was not ignored by the warlock.

Bad luck cosmically comes in threes, and problem number three was just dying for its fifteen minutes of fame, and its number was coming up.

26

"About Last Night"

Early that next morning Mrs. Weatherson had cereal, toast, fruit, pancakes, eggs and coffee ready for them. The cereal commercials at the time made it clear that these are the components to a well balanced breakfast. Uli and Ted were near crying of joy to have an actual breakfast for once, even in their normal status quo days, breakfast was something kids and old people got to partake in, coffee and smokes was the go to for the rest of the peons of humanity, them included.

All who had digestive systems stuffed themselves, and all who didn't (Oman) was jealous and heartbroken that he didn't get to try out those flattened cakes covered in syrup. He was a gourmand of sorts in his day, and witnessing such a spread made his brittle skull boil with envy.

They said their goodbyes and thanked Mrs. Weatherson for her hospitality.

After a small white lie about camping, they crammed

themselves into Mama W's van so as to not attract attention with Uli's affront to vehicular safety. Mom had a few days off and had no plans, she accepted the request for her ride under fear that the jalopy they rolled in on last night would blow up and get her little angel killed, the only request was not to get even a scratch on it, or she will have all their heads decorating her front lawn. The team believed her, her death gaze and monotone delivery of the threat made it easy to believe she would make them dig their own graves before decapitating them with a cheese knife.

With fear in their hearts they promised to get the old family car a good wash and a full tank when they get it back to her. They pulled out of the driveway narrowly missing the phalanx of trash cans next to the curve and made their way to the appropriately named *Blood Forest of Alzahar crater*.

In the momentary quiet of the start of the trip Carl found it odd that not one type of authority even bothered to call his house, he was working that night at Luminous Lakes Mall, you would think the mess they made would have made somebody pick up the phone. But survival logic prevailed in him, best not to dwell on things about to bite you in the ass till you can see its teeth. Etheria would be displeased with him for not thanking her for the good fortune she shined his way as of late.

It was way too early. The fog and minimal traffic on the back roads gave them a small but welcome sense of a road trip starting off on the right foot. Most of the team had fallen asleep again. The only two awake sipping coffee from giant thermoses was Ted on wheel and Uli in the copilot seat. Though fearful of letting Ted take the wheel, Carl was exhausted from last night and the adrenaline rush of telling a fib to his mother.

Uli looked to the backseat, getting a gander at the newly made fellowship of the two car garage. Carl had dozed off with Blood Fucker using the mall cop's thirty something beer gut as an ergonomic bed, while Oman seemed off in dream land himself. Reanimated skulls do not typically partake in mid morning siestas since the need of rest for recuperation was a curse only befallen to the living, but Oman was not ready to renounce all that made him human, he could in some form of meditation emulate the natural concept of slumber, he even managed to dream, which was most of the reason he made sure to get as close to the idea of sleep as he could, dreams are a blender of imagination, useful both for keeping one's creativity active and condensing magic in oneself, and in his limited state, he needed every ounce of the mojo he could grab hold too.

Ted saw a subtle but ice melting smile draw itself on Uli's face as she watched her band of the bizarre.
"What are you happy about?" Ted asked.
"A day ago we were stuck in a dead end world, and look at us now, a fully fleshed out party on a quest to an enchanted forest!" Uli said.
"Cursed blood forest Uli, the words you're looking for is cursed blood forest," Ted dead panned, with sitcom level accuracy.
"Yes cursed blood forest, but on a quest for justice dude! Like the heroes of old and shit."
"Oh a regular who's who of last picked fantasy role playing scrubs here." Ted added.

"I do enjoy the fact that I'm the one that looks like a vampire that lives in a cemetery, and YOU are the gloomy one in this enterprise," Uli said.

Ted loved and hated the fact bomb that blew up in his face, a brief laugh was shared until the car went silent, only the rhythmic combustion of the car saving them from absolute awkward silence.

"Do you remember what happened yesterday back at the mall?"

"The almost dying part? Yeah," Ted said.

"No, besides that, I mean when we were running up that forever staircase."

"I remember somebody falling, and well, my arm getting lasered off."

"And after that?" Uli asked.

"Can't say, I blacked out or something, moments of high stress can cause momentary amnesia I've heard."

"Yeah sure," Uli kept her demeanor calm and nonchalant, but hot flashes backed by flashbacks of Ted looking like he was possessed by the god of rough viking sex attacked her senses, she blushed instantly.

"You okay there Uli?"

Uli snapped out of it and looked to default Ted's schleppy face, the difference was so strong with his barbarian rock god alter ego she laughed out enough to almost wake up the peanut gallery in the back.

"What?" Ted asked.

"Nothing at all."

Ted shrugged and drank out of a dented thermos of coffee as they rolled down the road.

"I am truly sorry I dragged you into this." Uli said out of the blue.

"You mean grave robbing, participating in illegal magic and possibly overthrowing a world government? Nah I don't buy it, that sounds like every birthday gift you'll ever want all rolled into one, I don't think you're the least bit sorry."

"I really am, all this insanity, it's never been something you wanted from life and I knew it from the start. I've been pulling you through a fire you didn't start and that's not fair at all to you."

"Oh one hundred and one percent agree on that one," Ted fired with an honesty boosted delivery.

"I wouldn't blame you for leaving," she said with a sadness not at home in her usual peppy speech.

"I know."

"I mean you lost your job."

"Yup."

"And your arm at some point."

"Correct."

"And a demon possessed you for a second there."

"Yeah, no wait, what?!" Ted not aware that a creature from the underworld took a part of him for a test drive.

"And we could all die and nobody will be none the wiser." Uli said.

"Well besides the demon thing, I was present for all this, and as you can see I am still here."

"You're a people pleaser Ted," More of a Uli pleaser but I digress, "And that has exactly put you here, about to do even more crazy shit for me, I can't in good conscience put my best bud in any more danger, last thing I would ever want is to lose you, I take back the Ozen Maloique, you are free."

That last part hung in the air like a well fueled flatulence.

Every single ear in the back seat was listening with voyeur delight as they played sleepy sheep.

"Ted I..."

"Fuck you Uli," Ted said.

"I beg your pardon?"

"The nerve you walk around with on a day to day basis is awe inspiring, you know that? For such a tiny person you have an ego as big as the damn sword in the back," Ted added, "Nope, fuck you for every single word you just said."

Uli realized she had stepped in some dragon sized doodoo. "Why are you so mad?"

"You don't want to see me die?" Ted asked, frowning.

"Is that so bad?!"

"Yes it is! You said it with the dire certainty of it"

Uli was flabbergasted by Ted showing a spine, but the airs strike of righteousness was directed at her, and she was in no means a fan of it.

"How useless do you think I am that I'd be the first to go on this little horror show you managed to take on the road?"

"That is not what I meant Ted and you know it!"

"But that's how it felt! How do you think I would feel if my only friend, my best friend dies in the middle of a fucking blood forest and I did nothing? How will I live with that? Have you ever thought about that?" Ted said.

Uli hadn't. She felt like a guilt burrito torpedoed her gut with extra salsa.

"How dare you try to sideline me out of pity, what a trashy thing to do."

Uli was fighting off tears, her left nostril wanted to join in on the water snot deluge.

"So no Uli, Thank you very much. I think I will stay and help my friend, and show that I don't HAVE to die on a fucking suicide mission."

Face red, eyeliner running, cascades of tears running off her cheeks with every pout and sniffle, Uli was in shock.

Ted was winding up another therapy worthy haymaker, but he pumped the brakes on the verbal barrage he had released at his copilot.

A fusion of anger and love for his best friend festered in him. The tears from Uli made every door in his mind close shut to the idea of further hurting her feelings.

Uli saw her tears hit the fake leather seats, the thud of each drop echoed in the van. But the tone and texture changed in the drops, it was not tears falling now, it was blood, from Ted's nose.

She looked up to see Ted once again clad in the most stone chiseled of muscles, his nose broken (again) and bleeding, again his whole body covered in a lightning blue glow.

Whack! Bam! Boom! His eyes glowed in white hot fury. Ted kept one hand on the steering wheel and had the other pummel his face with punishing force.

The self inflicted pugilistic display awoke the fake sleeping imbeciles in the back seat.

"What the actual heck! What are you doing?" Carl screamed, "What is the meaning of this?" Oman added.

Ted had hurt Uli, and Ted cant stand for that, even from himself.

The road got choppy and was coming to an end, the perimeter fence stood no chance against the force of the battered vehicle, bashing it wide open to a trail that was by no means made for cars of such size.

Uli grabbed the steering wheel while Carl failed to restrain Ted's berserker rage.

"Snap out of it! We are running out of road!" Uli pleaded.

"Get his foot off the pedal!" Carl yelled, now sporting his very own nose bleed, courtesy of the back of Ted's head flinging back with each strike.

"I can't! He's too strong!"

"Blood Fucker, hit the breaks!" B.F. darted under the seats. Squirrels don't weigh all that much, so the minuscule minion had to put his weight into it. But he just wasn't heavy enough.

"What is happening? I can't see!" Oman yelled.

No trail left, they bounced into the light tree cover of the forest outskirts breaking every small tree in their path, the terrain was riddled with large stones and small drops, you could hear the car begin to fall apart.

"Ted listen to me, you are going to get us killed!"

Ted clobbered himself even harder.

Uli had a theory that was their only option as to not die wrapped around a tree. She timed her chance and jumped into the rain of punches, she hugged him and hoped she was right.

The incoming fist stopped inches from Uli's head.

Ted regained consciousness and put his foot on the breaks, squishing B.F. in the process, splattering him with extreme unintentional prejudice. The breaks did kick in, but the car began to slide on the centuries of accumulated loose gravel.

"We're not stopping!" Carl said, "Yes thank you, I can see that!" Uli yelled back.

A trio of timeworn boulders the size of large bears laid placidly before the oncoming station wagon. The front of the car met said trio with a thunderous steel crunch usually heard in crash test facilities.

***

The front of the car looked like an accordion. Every passenger smeared on the dashboard and fractured windshield.

"What happened?" Ted asked.

Carl, Uli and B.F. slapped, bit, punched and hair pulled Ted for the better part of a minute.

"Um, when you guys are finished, we should get our stuff and go, the crash is leaking and we don't want to be here if a spark hits anything flammable!"

Ted hoisted the sword out while Uli brought what she could out of the folded up car.

Uli looked at the very dead van.

"The car's dead now right? Can't you just bring her back?" asked Ted.

"I can, but the rebound from bringing the old girl back right now would konk me out for days." She looked at Carl, "I'll bring her back when we finish the job, I promise, I've done it before, I bet your mom's car has never been brought back before, so I can pull it off no problem, there's only so many times you can bring something back."

"How many times can you?" asked Carl.

"Never go past one," Uli said, to which Oman repeated the same.

"Why not?" Ted asked.

"Not enough there, something bad might happen after that."

"Like what?"

Uli with Oman in hand turned ominously to Ted, "Don't know, never tried."

"Me neither," followed Oman.

"We were going to have to go by foot soon anyhow, so let's call all that just happened a blessing."

"Yeah, but why though?" Ted asked. Carl pondered on an answer but opted to change the subject, as he was coming up blank to a proper answer to his confronted blind piousness.

"Look! We are almost at the start of the trail." Carl now proud of sticking the landing of changing the subject.

27

"Black Forest Jam"

A wall of black pine trees stood before them, and it's not that they were burnt, they had the bark, branches and pine needles of any old regular pine tree. But it looked as if somebody came in with a fire hose connected to a black paint factory and just drenched the whole place in the blackest of midnight. The closer they looked at them, they saw between the splits in the bark, a dark crimson sap bled from the cracks.

"Do you guys hear anything?" Carl asked.

"Like what?" Uli asked.

"No, I mean, like, do you hear anything?"

"Not a thing, hurry to the point acolyte I beg you," Oman said.

"All this woodland, and not a single cheep or chirp around," Carl Pondered.

"And what would that mean?"

"Either that the place is irradiated, or it's an enormous section of down wind terrain, or…" Carl activated woodland detective mode, "Ranger training tells me local animals don't feel all that safe here. And my faith tells me something in there is evil, and it doesn't particularly like guests this time of the year." all of them gulped, somehow even Oman did.

"Well let's get in and out before it knows we came to visit," Uli said with the deranged gusto of a seasoned adventurer.

"Oki doki sweety, time to do your thing," Uli shoveled Blood Fucker out of her bag and placed him on Dammerung, the blade did its usual fan fair and levitated just enough from the ground as to not disturb its surface. It swerved and swayed till it came to an elderly pace north east straight to the forest.

The squirrel-piloted sword made it to the tree line, every tree nearby hummed akin to throat singing from some far off mountain temple, only that it wasn't monks deep in prayer, it was some ungodly nightmare demon tree dirge.

"Well that isn't good," Carl said.

The hum mutated into a horrid heartbeat, they stopped in their tracks, Ted wasn't even in the forest yet, but he was fine with a carpet bombing or two leveling the whole place for good.

The heartbeat went louder and louder the further the blade made its unfaltering way in.

The trees visibly vibrated, the heartbeat hurried, Uli could swear she saw the trees begin to bleed,

The blade was almost fully in, if you still went on with the heartbeat analogy, it sounded like the forest was having a lethal heart attack.

Carl and Ted could now see the trees bleeding out in unison as well, covering the floor with a bright red, contrasting the black.

And then poof! The blood, the vibration, the throat singing, all gone.

Absolute silence took over again. They just stood there for a while looking at each other, coming to terms they just had their first shared hallucination.

Uli worded out, "What the fuck?"

"What the heck indeed?" worded Carl.

Ted was transfixed on the trees, mouth agape and eyes bulging. Uli nut tapped him, because friends are there for their friends. He slowly went to grab his family jewels, fell to the floor and curled up doing his best fetal position.

After being allowed to mourn his marbles, Ted got up and got one last look at the normal fields of the external perimeter they came in from, looking angelic in contrast to this surrealist hell intestine of the black forest ahead. He looked at Uli, her paper white face gave him a big dumb ass grin and waved him to "get in here!"

"Uli a word," Oman said, "Don't let any of the forest touch your bare skin."

"Oh I know, I get crazy rashes by anything with a leaf on it."

"No you fool, this place is filled to the brim with rotten magic, thousands of souls with no vessel, your underdeveloped necromantic attunement is an open door for them, one scratch from a branch and you'll be theirs for the taking."

"And you're telling us this now?" Ted said.

"I was not certain till I could feel it myself."

"Well that is a pickle now isn't it?" Carl said.

Uli flipped on her hoodie and tucked her hands into her long sleeves "That's a big ten four."

"Uli, we can't risk you." Ted said.

"We're here and I am dressed like a vampire going out on a summer day, I'll be fine, now shall we?"

She made her way in and all followed, and despite the general ambiance being dead quiet, everyone in the party could feel one thing for certain.

They had an audience…

28

"Burn The Rich"

Playing diplomat peace keeper was not Kalammet's favorite hat to wear. But he knew the name of the game well enough to keep this machine going, whether Volshtadt wanted it or not.

There he stood in the morgue under the capitol, looking at the supreme leader's massacre. Bodies now made to look like disturbing flesh made manhole covers filled the fridge, it was getting a lot more use than usual. He took it upon himself to inform the countries and protected states about the abrupt lack of life of the dignitaries sent to the anniversary.

They all took the news surprisingly well all things considered. He was sure the land of Voran Sammat would have something to say about a bloodline being erased, but not a peep or iota heard from the desert empire.

Last thing Kalammet wanted was an international incident that could spark up a war. But he was reminded how well a job they had done throughout the years in regard to stagnating any idea of rebellion, it just wasn't worth it. These leeches of the crown wouldn't last a fortnight, especially if Volshtadt decided to bring out his hell blade to the fray, whole countries would be thrusted into the abyss, it just wasn't worth the effort. But more impressively, the leaders of the modern age just loved the current world order, things worked for them, and if that means they have to bite the sacrificial bullet of some diplomats falling to Voldshtadt's blade, they could endure with moderate complaints.

The flattened bodies were thrown into the incinerator, not bothering to burn them one by one. Efficiency is the name of the game after all.

A thick cloud of smoke announced the approach of his most reliable and also most annoying of fixers.

Mr. Sundae stopped next to Kalammet and saw the royalty roast take flame. "Man, If I had known we're doing human sacrifice again, I would have shown up earlier," Kalammet snarled, quickly reminded how truly flawed and annoying the demigod community is, even the powers beyond have their black sheep he supposed.

"They must have said some nasty shit to have boss man go berserk on them."

"No, his majesty was simply bored." said the tired wizard, Mr. Sundae broke into a belly laugh. Again Kalammet wondered why such a simple thing like Mr. Sundae was gifted with demigodhood.

"His impulses are getting harder and harder to predict, one day he's functioning perfectly, then the next he's..." Kalammet waved at the human dinner plates, bones burning to ash as they watched.

"It's the sword ain't it?" Mr. Sundae asked.

"We cannot lose the course, our king is getting a case of sword induced immortal midlife crisis"

"The only thing that could kill him just came back from star gazing, I'm sure that causes a man such as the boss to ponder the possibility of ending it all."

Kalammet answered with silence.

"Still Haven't told him yet huh?"

Anger stirred inside Kalammet, It wasn't just because one of the most annoying deities ever to exist won't shut up. It was because the annoying nepo baby shithead was right.

Demigods are a rare and dying breed these days, having either died or just left the realm after the prophecy was broken. Faith was no more, belief, servitude, all to dust. It was said that the very god of creation just left, leaving reality to its own devices. Perhaps a rotting world had no appeal.

If the gods and their offspring cannot protect us from chaos, then what's the point in following them? Whoever of the pantheon that stayed had no choice but to descend and live with the humans and play nice with the meat bags that once knelt before them.

Mr. Sundae might have lost most of his powers as the god of smoke and whispers, but don't let that fool you, he could topple a government and take on its army on a slow weekend. But sustenance is required, and merc work is the quickest paycheck in town, especially the form of payment a warlock can provide.

"Be it some unknown fate, a cosmic joke the gods played for a millennia spanning jest, I won't have existence crumble to rubble because the cosmos itself is trying to pull one giant edit on reality! Now tell me where the sword is before I make a fire hot enough to burn a demigod."

"Slow your stride partner, it's on its way to the woods inside the Alzahar crater."

A fire in Kalammet's eyes burned brighter and far more ferociously than the incinerator before him, he did not want that sword in those woods.

"Get rid of it, take all the drakenstatz you can. but keep them on a short leash."

"That place is one of the last places with a good amount of joojoo juice, don't you think the dragon things are gonna react to it?" Mr. Sundae asked.

"A demigod is with them, I hope he has the power to control them, if not, what good is he? In fact what good was he ever?" Mr. Sundae isn't much for insults or slights, he grimaced enough to let the human know the low blow, but not enough to show it hurt.

Mr. Sundae's body turned to smoke, finding the closest vent to make its way back to his dormant body somewhere close to the woods.

Kalammet looked on at the final body to drop into the incinerator. He took in the sight of the dancing flames, he could feel the heat, the smell of a human being charred before burning to nothing. Something, somehow long ago broke the machine, and it felt like said machine was trying to repair itself, and his ancient resolve made it clear he'll burn everything to keep fate away from HIS kingdom.

29

"Hiking in Hell"

The fellowship of the garage followed the floating Dammerung through the forest. Its landscape put to shame the cover art of many a death metal band. But the forest was going to have to wait in line to drive them mad. Uli found the acoustics perfect to do a top twenty live countdown of her favorite Saturday morning cartoon intros from her childhood. Carl objected at first, but it seemed most wild life fled a while back, he let her carry on with her impromptu concerto. If anything, her tone deaf assault on the area probably kept any possible supernatural creepy creatures from getting closer, because nothing sane and healthy would ever make noises like the ones Uli was blasting out her mouth.

Ted was inoculated to Uli's killer vocals, he even joined in to harmonize on a couple. The only ones truly hating the experience was the two appointed mascots of the expedition.

"I have heard the predatory calls of demonic beasts that paralyzed the hearts of all the living things around them, I would welcome such ear raping roars if it would shut her up from what she calls a rendition of *Danger Dancers,* whatever the seven devils that is," Oman Zurr clamoured.

Blood Fucker did ponder the idea of ripping his ears out, but he felt it too disrespectful to his master.

Outside of the acid trip of a reception they got entering the forest, most of the hike so far was uneventful.

The unhallowed trees that looked as if they would impale you just for kicks got boring to look at after a few hours of seeing endless rows of the buggers. By the time they crossed their now third river of blood red water, the crew came to the collective consensus that the forest, if by chance, was a living entity itself, it was trying a bit too hard to come off as edgy. Even Carl's "all bark and no fright" pun got a couple of chuckles at the expense of the forest.

The sun was still visible through the trees, by its position it was well past noon, Ted suggested lunch and the group's rumbling stomachs concurred.

They found a lovely hellscape to sit at and have a round of Mrs. Weatherson's signature sandwiches. They stabbed the sword into the loose earth and used it as a coat hanger.

"To think this place had become such a graveyard. And just to be erased from time makes me a bit sad of how history is so quick to be let out to rot," Carl said, earnestly but still wanting to sound like a scholar waxing poetic.

"Oman, were you here during the war?" Uli asked like a fan girl to her favorite author. If Oman had muscles or skin, he would have had a smile from ear to ear.

"Two of them actually, what a playground it was for us Necromancers, so much raw product available, to have such a chance to exploit your potential was most gratifying," Carl gestured his faiths holy symbol over his body as to ward from the evil funk he felt Oman's words left in the air.

"In between the wars, councils argued over accords to limit necromantic participation in battles of a certain size. Mostly for the valid observations that it would prolong the carnage far longer than they needed to be. Necromancers would switch sides multiple times just to have twisted renditions of chess done with armies of corpses."

"Wait two battles? Was there more than one chosen one war? I'm officially confused." Ted asked.

"I apologize, just the one war, thousands of years get jumbled in this old bone of mine," Oman said, stumbling through his words.

"Bone." Ted chuckled.

Uli laughed at Ted's toilet humor, but glee faded away quickly to a sullen demeanor as she ate her sandwich.

"Miss Uli? Are you alright?" Carl asked, "Just Uli is fine Carl, just got lost in a thought there for a second"

"What is it? Spill it!" Ted said as he unwrapped his third sandwich.

"What if, you know, this whole thing goes south, then what? Nothing? We go back home, back to shit life, just now I'm missing an aunt?"

It was a question that had been on the mind of everybody, but Uli was the first to say it out loud.

"Oh no you don't, screw that!" Ted said, "Don't you dare get cold feet now! Now that we're halfway into the world's largest cemetery!"

"It's not cold feet okay?! Just, I mean, it's still a possibility. What if the hero isn't there? What if he is but it's just bones and dust? What if I don't have enough juice to bring him back?

What if..."

"Yeah, but what if you do?" Carl said, smiling as he slowly pulled out the thin onions his mother tried to sneak into his sandwich.

"What if you do have it in you? What if you do bring him back? What if we actually defeat Volshtadt? What if this restores the order of prophecy?"

"Yeah, that be cool but..."

"Miss Uli, every single thing we do everyday is a *what if...* What if we slip during a morning shower? What if the core of the planet turns to iron stopping its rotation and we all fall off the face of Thira?"

"That can happen? Well shit," Ted said.

Carl gave him his best apprehensive glare and tried to get back on his halftime speech.

"Point being, yes a million terrible things can happen at any moment to anyone, but we forget that a million good things can happen too. We get up, take our morning shower, go out into the world and hope the good things find us first."

"The sycophant is right," Oman said, "You forget you live in a realm where some magic still exists young lady, dozens of forces are pushing and pulling. You may not know the ultimate plan, but you just have to have a little..."

"Faith." Uli said with a grin. Carl felt like he converted a devil worshiper to the great Etheria, funny that he forgot that a talking possessed skull gave him an assist.

"There it is, faith!" Carl said as he rummaged through his duffle bag, "That reminds me of a pamphlet I have, maybe in the end, a path in the steps of Etheria is in your future."

"Nah, I'm good Carl, I haven't gone to church in ages."

"Do not rot the brain of my apprentice! You pamphlet

slamming Paladin!"

"Hey, when's the last time you ate Oman?" Ted asked, "You must be hungry, you haven't had anything to eat since you came back to the living." Ted went and grabbed the Skull.

"Where would I even put that peasant slop you git!"

"Come on, bet you miss the taste of food don't ya, here dude I'll help, I used to help my grandma eat when we would visit her in the old folks home on the weekend."

"Get back, do not touch me!"

Ted ignored the insults and put a piece of lettuce between the teeth of Oman and worked the jaw to make it look like the old skull was chewing. "There you go buddy, doesn't it taste good dude?"

"Insolence! Unhand me you brute! You are abusing the dead! Apprentice, tell your barbarian servant to unhand me at once!"

The fellowship got a good laugh out of it, but Uli felt the good natured ribbing had gone on long enough. "Alright Ted, leave Oman alone, I think he's full."

Ted stopped but felt his bit could have gone on at least a couple of more minutes. He placed Oman on the pine needle covered ground when Oman let out a panicked yell.

"Get me off the ground now!" Oman said, "I mustn't come into contact with the floor here! My affinity to it will attract too much attention from the forest." He wasn't wrong, no sooner he explained himself, the forest let out an earth rumbling moan.

Uli dropped B.F. and picked up Oman, the forest went silent once more. They all stood silent.

"I think we're in the clear," Carl said. Uli and Ted sat down relieved. Uli placed Oman once more on the sword's grip and added B.F. to the hilt.

"Why doesn't the forest react to Blood Fucker?" Uli asked.

"Undead he may be, but his signature is far too weak to get its attention."

Blood Fucker felt insulted by the forest, he was not ignorant of his size, but the jab still stung.

Oman powering it up, the sword reminded everybody that it maybe had a mind of its own and started floating its way north east.

"Come now follow me, it's leading us to the mountains," Oman commanded, giving off the enthusiasm of a child on his way to a theme park.

They picked up their picnic and followed the floating sword. Oman was finding himself amused at the fact that he had a vague avatar of a body.

Dammerung with its two stowaways moved on, not fast but never stopping, the fellowship found it increasingly difficult to keep up with the holy sword. Carl, though intensely devoted, did not appreciate the ever looping wind chime tune running through it. After a few hours it was now getting on everyone's nerves. You may say they are being a bit spoiled, but if you have someone hum next to your ear for two and a half hours, one might find the need to throw said singer back into space.

The day was in a rush to be over. Sunlight had worn out its welcome in the forsaken woods. The sun slowly went away and it was beginning to look obvious. They were not going to make it out of the woods that day. Carl with little to no help, set up a tent, got the fire going, and even got a pot of tea going, all in the span of twenty minutes.

30

"Decay"

Campsite was set and Carl was on his thirteenth patrol of the area, something that was getting on Ted's nerves. Meanwhile, Oman took it as a good opportunity to continue training Uli.

Close to the campsite they found a small dilapidated hut with most of its ceiling missing, the stone floor was optimal so as to not let the magic soaked soil interact with Uli.

She sat legs crossed, "So am I gonna summon some spears made of bones that float around me waiting to be flung? Curse something? Commune with dead guys?" Uli asked, jazzed up about getting another spell in her book from a legitimate Necromancer.

"Your youthful enthusiasm is only vaguely annoying," Oman said, "The magical well within you is very small at the moment, we have to make that well deeper and larger."

"Gross, You really have to work on your wording."

"Hush! You do have a unique aptitude for repurposing your revival necromancy, but you must learn how to take away as well."

"Meaning?" Uli asked. "I am meaning the art of DECAY!" Oman said.

"Ew." Uli muttered.

"Gross? Ew?! A Necromancer saying such things?! Blasphemous!"

"Sorry, just bringing spooky stuff from the ground and making creatures of the outerworld bend to my will is the cool stuff! The whole making something rot and die, it feels kind of wrong."

"If you do not explore every branch of your gift, how are you going to climb to the top of that tree?"

Oman was proud of the metaphor but saw it fly over Uli's head like an invisible arrow.

"Never mind, let us just decay then."

"Decay what?" Uli asked.

"Anything but the floor will do," Oman darted his eyes to a wall that was already half chewed up by the teeth of time.

"This wall would be a good start."

"Walls have life?" Uli pondered the possibility of living walls and was embarrassed by what her bedroom witnessed when she was in the more explorative moments of her womanhood.

"You have a mortal skewed view of it. It isn't just things that breathe and eat that live, to exist in the tangible world is to live."

Uli grasped a vague corner of the *waha pui* coming out of Oman, but she couldn't fathom the notion of a blender, a pencil or a mailbox being among the living.

"Like you did with your Theodore's arm, use your mind to reach out to the Eitherkreiss emanating from the wall, tap into it and make a bridge between the both of you."

"What's Eitherkreiss?"

"It's what we called in my time the raw product of magic that exists in all things, now close your eyes and find it calling to you."

"But I don't…"

"Don't what? Hear it? Feel it? Of course you don't, you never let the hole on your face shut up enough to actually listen, if you would stop your relentless nonsense and simply listen to the rotten, forgotten magic that dwells here, we may get somewhere with your training."

Uli wanted to snap back, but the beady lights in Oman gleamed with reprimanding pressure. She thought it best to close her mouth and listen to her *Sensei* of a skull, for now.

She shut her mouth, closed her eyes and relaxed doing her best to imagine tendrils of black dance out of her aura, reaching for whatever was willing to make contact.

Stagnant energy hung heavy in and around the building, reacting to the presence of Uli and their shared death soaked affinity, the building slowly reaching out to her. Echoes of long past memories reverberated from its essence, as would an old man wanting to share his story to anybody willing to listen.

"Yes, there it is," Oman said.

Uli focused on the wall, "Eitherkreiss serves to manifest in reality what your attunement allows you to imagine. See every structural part of the wall, the wood, the mud, the rock, now in your mind's eye see it decay."

Uli knew that the better the imagination, the better the magic. But still, it was a hell of a hurdle to break the barrier of logic that separated her inner and outer world. That is where spoken spells came to assist. Spell names are keys to unlock a specific action.

When the components are placed and mixed in the right way, it will allow the spell user to know the right key.

A subtle wind picked up in the hut, sesame sized bits of clay started to fall out. Cracks began to form making grooves all around the surface of it. Syllables echoed inside the room.

"Good! Good! You're finally listening!"

The words swirled around her like a playful ghost, half in her imagination, half in reality, she was manifesting a pocket space of altered reality where magic can happen.

Then just like that. It popped into her head...

Elam Shumaak...

"Say it!" Oman shouted within the swirling vortex of magic. The words swelling like balloons in her brain."

Uli spoke the words, chunks of wall crashed down around them, the smell of mold filled the vacant living room, rocks corroding to dust, a book sized section in the upper left corner of the wall aged thousands of years in an instant.

"Very good young lady," Oman said, "Again."

"But I just showed I could do it, no need to...*blourf*!" Uli regurgitated the black ink substance followed by losing her balance and landing on her backside.

"Your body has no tolerance for the rebound, how do you expect to survive a fight if you are spilling your insides with every incantation? Now clean your face, spit out the rebound and do it again!"

Uli sniffled for only a second, she puffed out a grunt and stood herself up to deepen her well of magic.

***

Ted could hear Uli's training, every brick he heard tumble made his face light up like a proud parent. Carl saw the wholehearted reaction and put up a smile of his own.

"You guys are really close huh?" Carl asked.

"Guess so, neighbors since kids, she would see me in the front yard playing with my toys. She was always asking to join in. It took a few days of bugging me until I gave in. She won me over cause she would always let me win."

"That was nice of her."

"Sure, but then her guys would come back like toy zombies, I agreed she can do that, but only once per game."

"You and your Mom are super close right?" Ted said.

Carl chuckled, "We are, Mom used to be super religious, my Dad got her into the faith of Etheria. When he passed… she just stopped praying. She couldn't bring herself to believe anymore, but it didn't bother her that I kept at it. She said it reminded her of Pops."

Despite his casual way of responding, Ted could still hear the scarred up but present pain Carl carried for his father.

"How'd he go? Your dad I mean."

"He was a beat cop, responded to a break in. The robber had a gun, some poor junkie, desperate, first break in most likely, he was jittery, he pulled the trigger. After he shot my dad, witnesses say he started crying. They got my dad to the hospital. He was there a few days before he passed away." Carl pulled the amulet out from under his shirt, "Before he went he gave me this, told me not to be angry at the man who did this."

"Dude, how could you not though?" Ted asked.

"My thoughts exactly, but he said that Paladins don't hate the man who does evil, we fight the evil that broke them!"

Ted shook his head "Heavy shit."

"Heavy poop indeed," Carl answered.

"Is that why you wanted to be a cop?"

"Police, highway patrol, military, park ranger, nobody would take me."

"Why not? You're like super smart and helpful."

"I always failed the psych evaluation, I know I could have cheated my way through them and just said what they wanted to hear, but it didn't feel right."

"Why would you fail? You seem pretty normal to me, all things considered…" Carl shook his amulet.

"Religious prejudice? Shit you could sue them!" Ted said.

"I know what I look like to the non-believers. When they went into the *what if?* Questions like 'What if you have to save a little girl or five men stuck in a fire pit?' They got incredulous every time I said the goddess would guide me to the answer when the time was right," Ted nodded at the thick religious nut spread Carl was sharing out, "They felt my faith fogged my ability to take action or responsibility.

Ted nodded, slurped the last of his tomato soup and heard Uli's continued desecration of an archaeological site. "Well, I guess all this is a proof of concept of sorts," Ted said.

"What is?"

"You're here, helping a Necromancer use taboo magic to kick start a prophecy that's been dead for thousands of years. I don't know much about faith, but if every little decision and happenstance that occurred in your life led you to one day become a mall cop, and then placed you at that mall the same time we showed up, and then you appeared when we needed you the most, and now you're here Mr. Paladin, that looks like divine providence to me, don't you think?"

Carl was pleasantly stunned by Ted's monk-like eloquence. Insight comes from unexpected places.

"Amen to that," Carl said.

"Amen dude," Ted responded, "Now if you could use some of that holy mojo to get us out of here it be super nice."

"Agreed, those trees freak me the heck out."

"It's like they are creeping up on us or some shit."

"It may look like that, but it's only because the forest is so dense," Said a voice coming from a dense bunching of trees."

Ted and Carl both stood up, Carl wasting no time to unsling his thick flashlight aiming it at the intruder. There stood a portly man well into his fifties, his wide brim ranger hat went out over the shoulders of his well ironed uniform.

"Easy gunslinger, put that solar flair of a flashlight down."

"Who are you?" Ted asked, wielding a spork like he meant business.

"Name's Ranger Harry Hamlock, I'm in charge of this quadrant, and it appears to me you two are trespassing on a national park well out of camping season. You two have anything to say for yourselves?"

Carl deactivated the light as his eyes met with Ted, both searching for an answer. Ted found one but his quick thinking did not manifest a good answer, only perhaps an honest one.

"Um, uh, sorry? Yeah, just sorry sir."

Ranger Hamlock let out a belly jiggling laugh, he brushed his thick mustache and approached the boys with a walk that was more of a waddle.

"Tell ya what, you give me a bowl of that there soup and you tell me what you two gentlemen are doing here and maybe I'll let this little intrusion slide."

Ted and Carl shared another silent stare at one another and nodded.

"How can we be sure you're a Ranger?" Carl asked.

"Fare question, but do you think some old yahoo would get into a Ranger costume and walk around in this horrible place just for kicks unless he was paid to do it?"

The comment went unanswered for a moment, Carl secured his flashlight back to his belt.

"Hope you like tomato soup," Carl said, admiring how well the uniform looked, even on the out of shape protector of the forest before him.

"Oh I could swim in the stuff." Hemlock answered.

31

"Tag Team"

Uli stood hunched over, hands anchored at her knees, the floor stained by the darkened magic puke. The dry heaving had stopped, but her body let her know that if she had any other ideas outside of sleeping, it was not going to cooperate.

"Playing both the clay and the sculptor takes its toll, you are not only manipulating Eitherkreiss, you are using your mind, body and spirit to build a bridge into reality, that's why it takes such a strain, only beings such as humans with vast imaginations are capable of this process, that is why they need you."

"Who? Like people, the greater good and crap?" Uli asked.

"Oh... er, um, yes! Correct, greater good, yes very good!"

"There, you did it again, that, you redirected an answer and stuff."

Oman diverted his eyes, embarrassed on being caught so simply, he found out that thousand year old ghost brains aren't as quick as their corporeal counterparts. He sighed, "Young

Uli, there are things at play far more complex than reviving a prophecy."

"I get that, saving humanity, freedom, justice and getting fate back on the rails, it's serious shit, scary yeah, but I can take it."

"I wish it was that simple, but since I came back I have noticed that certain pieces in the greater machinations of Thira are missing, have been missing for a long time. What we have embarked on puts certain parts in movement once more, but I fear what might come, both possible outcomes have risks, I am seeing to the one that has the less danger."

"You've only confused me and added a layer of dread on top of it."

"If we succeed and we are still alive by the end of it I promise to explain, no sense compounding the weight of our current endeavor, let us simply focus on the task at hand, once on the other side I believe you will be ready to know the greater cogs of what will come."

Uli didn't like being left in the dark, but did appreciate the fact that she did not have enough space for another boulder on her back, one clusterfuck at a time is fine by her. She nodded as she went upright and wiped off the drying tears from her black gut spilling rebound session.

"Alrighty, so resurrection, how are we doing this?"

"The fact your squirrel hasn't exploded yet shows you know the spell well enough, it's the same exact ritual, but this will require far more power. If I was whole I could have done it myself, but we work with what we have, so you are going to have to straddle me."

"Hell no perv!"

"It means to piggyback."

"Oh, then say piggyback, you don't have to sound like you're wired to a dictionary all the time."

"Your limited plebeian vocabulary is not the issue at hand."

"Now you're just being rude."

"You have to piggyback me to make dead important man not dead anymore."

"See? Was that so hard? And how do we do that?"

Oman rolled the small flickers of light were his eyes should be, "Your Eitherkreiss and mine will cycle between us and meld enough to complete the spell, the words and ritual are no different, but we are dealing with the unknown of tampering with a chosen one, we should expect, perhaps a glitch or two."

"Such as?" Uli asked, Oman stayed silent.

"Spill it skull boy!"

"This has never been done, we are tampering with a being touched by fate, who knows what such meddling could cause, all we can do is try and hope for the best."

Uli was used to uncertainty, it kept life exciting, but Ted's paranoia had rubbed off on her when it came to such world altering circumstances being left to a "let's see what happens."

"Now let's see if you can down the whole building, after that you can rest and get some supper"

"The whole building?"

"Yes child, the whole building."

Uli pouted as she set herself up for another round of decay when an inhuman sound came from the camp.

"What is it?" Oman asked.

"Nothing, thought I heard a turkey fighting a dolphin…"

32

"Stranger Ranger Danger"

Ranger Hamlock slurped his soup through his mustache, with every spoonful he grunted and moaned like a man that hadn't had a meal in a good long while. Carl was proud that his mother's skills in cooking pleased a man of the badge, Ted on the other hand found the pleasure-drenched noises coming from the portly guest where a bit too similar to the ones found in certain films that only rich folks with cable had access to after midnight. During the soup slurp session, Hamlock would give Dammerung a gander.

"Man I tell you, whoever made this better be married, cause if they ain't, imma have to see how to put a ring on that finger."

"I'll let my mom know you liked it, but she is getting serious with her current boyfriend."

"Shame, but if she ever is available, tell her old Harry would be honored to hand her some flowers before a nice steak dinner."

"I will sir, thank you."

"Made a polite one out of you, she raised ya right. You two brothers?"

Ted and Carl looked at each other and gave a small chuckle.

"No, just friends." Ted said.

"Now, you two are about two minutes from being off the hook, but I still gotta ask due to my inquisitive nature why y'all picked such a hell hole for a brotherly camping trip?"

Ted could lie his posterior off till the sun came up with the greatest of ease, but he tensed knowing that the boy scout sitting next to him had a harder time telling a fib than breathing under water. He had to think fast before Carl felt the annoyingly natural need to never tell a lie.

"Myth hunters! We are um, Myth Hunters yeah, we've been going around all over the place looking for proof of those monsters people say they saw and stuff, came in here looking for a big old man looking thing made out of dirt and tree branches."

"Oh? Haven't heard that one before, has it got a name?" Ranger Hamlock asked, not a pebble of sarcasm in his tone.

"Yeah of course, the ancient mythical TREE GUY," Ted said.

A heavy awkward silence took over the campsite, as if the forest itself became paralyzed by the sheer unoriginal dog shit Ted produced with the answer.

Carl Eyed Ted, wondering if his height caused a less than optimal flow of blood to his brain.

"Oh yeah not just a Tree Guy, THE Tree Guy, nine feet tall, eyes like a goat, when he walks you could hear him miles away, likes to eat kids that run away from home, they say he can camouflage like a tree and grabs the little runts and eats them then and there, some say he was born of nuclear waste falling on a homeless man while living out in the woods, the only way you know you're in the right place is when it lets out its terrible warning call."

Carl in incredulous awe on how is it that a whole backstory pulled out of some drunk author's failed fairy tale burped out of Ted, but all he could conjure up was calling it a Tree Guy.

Forest Homunculi, the Woodrian Demon Dwarf, heck! The Forest Dweller, even Carl could come up with more believable titles, but as he processed he looked at Hamlock, and the Ranger never stopped drinking his soup.

"Well damn, and how does that warning call sound like? Been here a while, maybe I've heard it."

Carl now turned his head to Ted, his eyebrows high saying with the gesture, "Well you big moron, now what?"

"Go on now tiny, sing it for me and maybe I can point you in the right direction."

Ted didn't hesitate, his jaw went down, he readied his lungs and let out a sound that could only be compared to a castrated bear throwing up a barns worth of panicking turkeys. He did this sound far longer than necessary, sweat had coated Carl's back and arm pits, cold against his skin from the now cooling night.

Hamlock stopped eating, seemingly entranced by Ted's odd acapella. Ted finally ran out of breath and closed his mouth, staring straight at the Ranger. Hamlock stretched his grin so wide it escaped the confines of his broom-like mustache.

"Welp, can't say I've heard that around these parts, but then again maybe the Tree Guy didn't want me finding him out."

"Oh they are sneaky bastards, but we'll catch him, you'll see."

Hamlock laughed as he put his bowl on the ground, "You're a nutty critter ain't ya Tiny, I like you."

He laughed for so long that the boys felt obliged to join in,

Ted with a rather well realized fake laugh, when Carl started he sounded like he was reading out loud "ha ha ha" from a book to the class.

Hamlock pat around his body looking for something.

"Well I do hope you boys find that Tree fella, maybe I can be there when you do and get a bit of the limelight."

Ranger Hamlock found what he was looking for in his jacket pocket, a fancy cigarette container.

Ted and the Ranger kept on laughing, Carl went quiet, eyes squinting as Hamlock brought out a large copper plated lighter and sparked up an odd looking cigarette.

"How long have you been a Ranger officer Hamlock?" Carl asked.

"Oh not enough to retire, but long enough to forget when I started."

"Are you up to date with the Ranger guide book?"

"Know it like the back of my hand." He said as he lit his smoke, taking a long drag from it, but looking right at Carl through the smoke, Ted realized that his still continued laugh was not welcome in the change of conversation and shut up.

"Then you would remember page twelve subsection two regarding Ranger etiquette and safety while in a wooded area."

Hamlock tapped on his smoke, ash falling to the blackened earth, he let the smoke leave his nostrils like a ghostly cascade.

"Oh damn, you caught me, never could remember that one part, why don't you do me a favor and jog my memory."

"It states that Rangers be they on duty or not, must not under any circumstances partake in cigarettes, cigars, pipes or any fire based recreational substance if they are within or close up to a five hundred yard proximity of a wooded area, not only to maintain the public image of a law enforcement officer, but also for the obvious fire hazard implications."

Hamlock dropped his cigarette and stomped it out with his heavy boot, "You guys have a fire, doesn't that book say something about that?"

"It does, it says to rid the area of dry leaves and branches, dampen the location, build a fire pit and maintain the fire to a manageable burn so as to not have flames catch nearby branches, all which has been properly done since establishing this place as our campsite for the night."

Now it was Ted's turn to give Carl the raised eyebrow treatment, confused as to why Carl was now treating the jolly and jiggly Ranger to an impromptu oral exam.

Hamlock pulled out another cigarette and lit it as he broke his gaze on Carl.

"You're no fun, why cant you be more like Tiny over there, spitting nonsense that smells worse than the bullshit that bullshit shits out from eating shit, at least he's entertaining, I was so close to just letting you two idiots get out of here if you gave up the pig sticker over there and the girl that dresses like a hooker at a funeral, but you had to get all technical on me."

"Who are you?" Carl said as one hand went to clench his amulet while the other went to his skull cracker flashlight.

"Oh I got a whole laundry list of names you folk gave me throughout the years, I would be obliged to tell ya, but no sense in that now is there?"

Rustling bushes sound all around them followed by a reptilian guttural rattle, quick shrieks of a platoon's worth of dragonsacks.

Ted looked around and found a dozen glowing eyes floating in the darkness like fireflies.

Carl gasped, Ted looked back at Hamlock to find the Ranger

dissipating into multicolored smoke, revealing a thin man with dirty blond hair and a smile much too long to fit on a human face.

"Real shame, I was starting to like you two," Mr. Sundae pointed to Carl, "Gonna have to kill you." He then points to Ted, "I am going to let the dragon boys back there eat the big one, then throw that there sword into outer space and get rid of your witch friend, so if y'all kindly just sit there and let us do our thing, everything can go back to normal and I can go back to my shows."

"In Etherium Sanctum!" Carl yelled grabbing his amulet with his left hand, with his right he unsheathed his flashlight, a surge of yellow light engulfed his left arm, the current of light transferred to the flashlight, he aimed at Mr. Sundae, turned it on bursting forth a beam of light brighter than the sun engulfing the demigod, its incandescence filled with righteous holy fury, the overflow hit a couple of the dragonsacks incinerating them while blinding the rest in its radiant splendor.

"Get Uli and the sword out of here! I can take em!" Carl yelled, adrenaline and faith coursing through him, giving him the elated bravery of a holy man on a battlefield thwarting evil.

Ted was about to bolt when he saw Mr. Sundae rush to Carl escaping the holy light, the demigod grabbed Carl by the wrist, applying enough pressure to make him release the flashlight , but not enough to break it.

"Nice party trick kid, But Etheria's light show can't hurt other gods, or demigods for that matter, only thing you're doing is giving me a nice tan."

Ted froze, debating his next move, one choice being to just get murdered and finally be out of this hamster wheel of shit he's been stuck in. His legs finally decided to move towards the now captured Carl, his charge on Mr. Sundae was made short by three dragonsacks cutting him off.

Mr. Sundae lifted Carl from the wrist, holding him like he just caught himself a big one from the fishing hole. He looked at Carl with a casual curiosity, "It's always a treat to find one of Etheria's sheep roaming around this forgotten rock, it's so embarrassingly funny to see y'all waive your hands and chant like something was actually listening."

"Shut up devil! You're just trying to confuse me, Etheria listens and protects us! The power of the amulet is proof of it!"

Mr. Sundae blew a cloud of smoke right into Carl's face, the smoke so thick and toxic it burned Carl's lungs with the sting of a chemical fire.

"I hate to break it to ya holy boy, but little Miss Glitter Pants or anybody for that matter ain't listening, not for a long time, the only reason that cheap toy on your neck is glowing is just leftover mojo from when the bitch was still around."

Carl saw despair in Mr. Sundae's eyes, the words coming from the demigod sounding like an angered child that was never picked up from school. The god of whispers couldn't hide the hurt of being left behind. The truth in the words hit Carl hard, his whole life, his faith questioned thousands of times from a myriad of men and women, but it wasn't till this moment, dangling from the arm of a magical being that his core of belief was impaled by a javelin.

"Liar!"

"Don't hate the messenger kid, just wanted to let ya know before you die that no shiny hot piece of ass is on the other side to show you to your table, you'll just be dead, sorry about that."

Mr. Sundae blew out a thin plume of smoke to his free hand, in an instant solidifying into rough steel, its tip as sharp as a needle, "No hard feelings kid."

"Elam Shumaak!"

The spell echoed through, Mr. Sundae searched for the source of the words but felt something odd, something, small, something ignored but always vital for the ability of running, walking and especially staying upright just disappeared from his body, his left Achilles heel crumbled to dust, "Oh boy," Mr. Sundae tried keeping his balance, but it's hard while holding up a grown man with one arm, he fell to the dirt hard, Carl's body tumbling over him, the utility belt strapped to him scratched and smashed Mr. Sundae's entire face as he rolled over.

A decay spell came to visit Mr. Sundae, but only powerful enough to putrefy one single solitary tendon, but at that moment that was all Uli could kill, but that was all she needed.

The small scraping with the mortal feeling of pain shook Mr. Sundae, though not a stranger to the favorite sensation of many a masochist, he could count with one hand the times he ever actually felt the horrid censorial sting, and needless to say he was not a fan.

Carl rolled away springing back in a kneeling fighting stance, night stick in hand, flash light in the other, Carl was tired but ready to impart some divine justice.

Ted caught a break when the team of dragonsacks stopped and directed their attention to the source of the spell.

Uli stood proud, Oman tucked under her right arm and

B.F. on her shoulders, she donned a purple lip glossed smile, though now covered in black vomit and her knees shaking, she did her best to look as bad ass as she thought she looked in her imagination.

"Uli!" Ted ran to her, noticing her pale skin was near transparent now, Oman had pushed her too far in training, the last spell she shot was already produced with only the vapors of her inner Eitherkreiss.

Dragonsacks sprinted her way, Ted making it to her side safely thanks to Carl shooting his holy flashlight beam cannon on the beasts, the mutated quasi-dragon kin bursted into white hot flames. The vile Eitherkreiss eaters could consume near infinite amounts of any magic in the realm, but laying a dose of holy light on them was the equivalent of giving a dog a double fudge chocolate milkshake sprinkled with cyanide and garlic. Ted grabbed her shoulders tight.

"You okay?" Asked Ted.

"Okay? I just saved you and Carl's ass with magic, hell yeah I'm good!" With that last word he felt her knees buckle, he would have kept her up regardless but the terror of her making contact with the exposed forest was an added safeguard.

"Wow there." Ted said.

"She's exhausted, I should not have pushed her," Oman said.

"Oh you think?!"

"Chastise me later! We need to get her out of here!"

Ted's right hand whipped up catching a darkened gray spear shot right at Uli's left eye, it dissipated to smoke when it didn't reach its destination. Eyes bright with an electric blue hue, Ted turned around to see Mr. Sundae back on his feet, his right ankle engulfed in gray smoke binding it up enough to stand.

"The party is just starting boys and girls," Mr. Sundae shot smoke out both his nostrils, the double streams found his hands, equipping him with two more smoke spears. He wasted no time launching them with superhuman precision. Ted hugged Uli to his now rock hard chest, Uli offered no resistance, both from weakness, and not being per say bothered by being pressed onto a washboard stomach.

Ted leapt away from the spears, landing so hard and heavy that the earth shook as if Ted weighed a metric ton.

"Big boy's got tricks too huh?!" Mr. Sundae prepared another volley, he saw from the corner of his eye the sword completely unattended. He launched a single smoke spear at Uli. Ted leapt once more, dodging it by a hair. In the distraction Mr. Sundae dashed for the sword, he held it by the grip but the Dammerung reminded the demigod that it was picky on who got to work the grip, burning his hand as it once scorched Volshtadt's long ago.

"You holy son of a bitch!" His smoke spear broke down to its ethereal floating form engulfing the sword levitating it in mid air.

Carl was busy slaying dragons and loving it, but both he and Uli saw Mr. Sundae about to steal the sword.

"Don't need to kill y'all, sword's enough for now."

"No!" Uli screamed.

"Wait what's happening? Oh crap, I did it again didn't I?" Ted phasing out of his trance.

"Elam Shumaak."

Uli focused the last of her magic to one more decay spell, aiming for the smallest target she could concentrate on, a single half rotted tooth. She spoke the words and Mr. Sundae let out a scream that startled even the dragonsacks who were still battling Carl. The smoke dissipated and the sword fell.

"Way to go Uli!" yelled Carl.

"Yeah good going dude, but I thought you were out of…" before Ted could finish the sentence he heard Oman scream as Uli dropped him, she immediately followed, her hands dulled the impact before her face met the cursed earth of the blood forest.

"Noooooooo!" Oman yelled.

She was only exposed to the raw ancient death of the land for a second before Ted picked her up like a limp rag doll, but that instant became eternal within Uli, thousands of souls coursed through her, spilling their memories of warfare and blood filled demises. Warriors and fallen wizards, their rotten stagnant Eitherkreiss overcharging her, her eyes flipped back and her body violently shook, screams from thousands of different errant souls roared out of her bringing to the battle a wave of death rattles. None were safe from the attack. Every single able bodied creature close to her was paralyzed in pain.

Carl took advantage of the maddening scream and powered through to the sword, dragging it away from Mr. Sundae and his minions.

"We have to get her and the sword out of here!"

"What?" Ted screamed, "I said we have to get her and the sword out of here!"

"What?" Ted said once more, unable to hear the paladin.

Carl screamed frustrated, when he reached them he picked up Oman and Blood Fucker and placed them on the sword powering it up to make its unhurried exit, Ted getting the gist of it carried Uli out as he followed Dammerung into the pitch black forest.

Uli screamed while they retreated, "Shut her up! She's

just calling them over for dinner if we don't get her to stop screaming!"

"If I knew how to do that Carl I would have done it by now wouldn't I?"

The forest provided the solution with Ted accidentally bumping Uli's head against a tree. She went silent.

"Fuck sorry Ul's!" Ted's right fist found its way to his right eye in retaliation for accidentally hurting her.

"At least she stopped," Carl said. Uli may have stopped her painful call but they both forgot that the sword enjoyed doing its wind chimed melody as it floated along.

"Oh yeah, that, plus it's moving like it's sightseeing." Carl said.

Branches broke and roars arose behind them. "We have to slow them down, Uli and the sword are the only ones that have to reach Aiden!" Carl said.

"She's not in marathon shape dude!"

"Stop!" Carl removed Oman and B.F. and placed them aside, the sword sticking itself into the loose dirt.

He then removed his flashlight, nightstick and taser from his belt, unbuckled it, sliding it off in a hurry.

"Quick, put Uli's back to the sword!"

"What the hell are you doing!" Ted asked.

"Do it! I'm trying to get her out of here."

Ted did so and Carl wrapped his belt under Uli's arms then locking it over the cross guard of Dammerung, Uli hung from the belt like a wrestler knocked out over ropes of the ring. Carl looked at Oman and Blood Fucker, "It's up to you two to get her there in one piece, We'll try to catch up, but if we don't, you know what to do."

"You have my word," Oman said with a tone of respect he

never gave to the mall cop, B.F. chitted the same oath. Carl nodded and placed them on the sword's grip and cross guard. Dammerung levitated once more, not bothered with the added weight of Uli, it floated on to its final destination.

Ted and Carl saw Uli float away with the soothing light of the sword emanating around her. In Carl's eyes the sight felt brimming with religious iconography worthy of any church sermon. For Ted it looked like he was never going to see his friend again.

Carl shoved a knife in Ted's left hand and the nightstick in the other, "I'm going to need you to go into that glow stick mode of yours, that's the only way we are going to help Uli."

"I don't know how to turn it on dude! It just happens!"

"No it doesn't!" Carl slapped Ted hard, "A circus worth of freaks are coming for your bestest best friend, do you think they are just going to take the sword? They need her dead and fast, they know what she can do and the only way to stop it is getting rid of her the second they see her, they make it through us and they will kill her! So DO YOUR FUCKING JOB and protect your friend."

Ted returned the slap to Carl so hard his ears rang and his jaw nearly dislocated. Ted growled at him, making the would-be ranger's holes pucker up. Guardian Ted was engulfed in blue energy as he walked towards the roars.

Carl spat out a tooth, gripped his flashlight and taser, "That's more like it."

33

"A Lazy Escape"

The battle waged on behind them, flames engulfing the trees. Oman could not reach out with his mind to the others, the screams of the dragonsacks and the constant explosions of fire breath was a good thing, if anything he feared absolute silence. The odds were not on Ted and Carl's side. Let the war rage on as far as he was concerned. He was now only the hood ornament on the sword, helpless to the constant momentum of Dammerung. Uli was not waking up anytime soon, she was stuck in her own private nightmare at the moment.

Blood Fucker squeaked in worry over his master.

Oman did not have the heart to tell him of the torture and possible death of Uli. The undead Necromancer was feeling empathy? That one concept scared him, he was sparing a squirrel from a sorrowful moment. Developing empathy was not something on his vision board. Spending too much time with this parade of buffoons was now rubbing off some good nature, and gods forbid cheer into him. If he had had a gag reflex he would have triggered it then and there.

But Uli was busy in a battle for her own mind and body, who knows how long she could hold out.

Oman could have helped if he was whole and not rationing what little magic he had left.

Oman was once the terror of Thira, long before posers like this Volshtadt fellow and that young upstart Kalammet, Now his life only a creepy party trick. Deep in thought he didn't notice the blade stopped moving, or Blood Fucker knocking the top of his head.

"Stop that you wretched beast! What are you bothering about?!"

Blood Fucker twirled Oman on the grip of the sword to get a good view of what was stopping them. Tendril-like branches had wrapped around Uli's legs straining the high tensile strength of Carl's utility belt.

"Drat!" Oman said, the forest got a taste of Uli and wanted some more.

"Release her! I command you!" The branches did not oblige. Looming above, the sharp branches of the bleeding trees arched towards them with menacing intent. They not only had to contend with that smoke wizard and his dragon pets, now the very land they walk wants them.

Gurgled, sloppy combinations of gut churning sounds brought his attention back to Uli.

The toxic fumes of acid brought his line of sight to the splotches of acid on the branches, Blood Fucker was on the attack! The forest moaned in pain as the char colored branches rotted and stretched till they went *snap*!

B.F. spewed away all the acid he could to save Uli.

"You wonderful disgusting thing, keep going!"

He didn't have to tell Blood Fucker twice, he was tiny and easy to step on, but he still could do something, and he was willing to spill his toxic guts on the whole forest if he could, he was going to save Uli no matter what. The acid drenched branches snapped releasing Dammerung back on track.

"Well done rodent!" The tiny terror rejoiced of his momentary victory, his acid reserve near empty.

Oman commanded the exhausted B.F. to spin him around as the never ending encroaching of the forest continued all around them, dozens upon dozens of roots and branches bursting out the ruined soil.

B.F. climbed on top of Oman spitting out his streams of acid in every direction, his cyclonic defense of the moving perimeter was working, but every squirt of bile became thinner with every belch. B.F.'s already corroded state progressed further, ribs protruding, void space where his belly should have been. Oman knew the little warrior could only keep this going a moment longer before they were swallowed whole by the forest, never to be seen again.

Oman saw before them one thing that could stop Dammerung enough for the forest to claim its prize, impeding their path was a gargantuan tree, trunk thick as a load bearing pillar, its own branches reaching out for them like a spider waiting for its food.

B.F. tumbled off of Oman "Blood Fucker!" the squirrel fell, body wedging between the sword and Uli's neck. The forest reached out, the trunk of the tree shaking with anticipation for its feed.

Uli could barely reach out to the waking world, the cyclone of souls swallowing her sanity, but she felt her familiar in danger, all she could say was, "Blood Fucker, good boy…"

* * *

If you have never heard a squirrel roar, it's pretty adorable. Such a whimsical woodland creature capable of a war cry is awe inducing and heart melting all at once. Truth be told they do not roar, but Blood Fucker gave it his best try that night. He jumped down to the ground, getting between Dammerung and the unmoving tree and let out his war cry. It sounded like white noise from a television at full volume.

"What the hell are you doing?!" Oman said.

No hesitation in Blood Fucker's eyes, he shot his tiny clawed paw into his stomach stabbing as deep as he could, he gripped his intestine and pulled it out, not once wincing or looking away from the tree.

"My word, it's gone mad," Oman said, not far from the truth. Vengeance boiled in B.F.

He squeaked on as he sprinted in a berserker's fury, snagging the tip of his intestine to a small jagged edge on the base of the evil pine tree, he ran around it at top speed, his guts spilling out like a slimy miniature fire hose, the moment his guts made contact on the trunk, fumes burned from its bark. The forest bellowed in pain, he managed two full laps around the tree before he ran out of his corrosive innards, he gripped his insides and pulled as hard as his necrotic muscles could muster. The lunacy of his actions caught up to him, his brain realizing what occurred and zapped his nerves with pain. Blood Fucker did not have time for the pathetic notion of pain, he pulled on, digging his intestine deep into the tree. Oman witnessed on as Uli, Dammerung and himself snailed their way on to their demise, now only feet away from it.

"You can do it little one, do not stop!" never had Oman seen such loyalty and devotion from a familiar to its master. Most familiars had nothing but contempt to the wizards that shackled them into service. But Blood Fucker was not only ready to die, but do it in the most heroic bad ass way the Necromancer had ever seen.

Layer by layer the trunk broke down by the caustic substance. The sword was only inches from the tree, the lowest branches now at arms length from reaching Uli. One more touch of the forest would collapse Uli's mind rendering Blood Fucker's efforts a fool's errand.

"Wake up Uli! Open your eyes or we'll be done!"

Uli, a prisoner of her mindscape, could hear Oman's words out in the infinite distance beyond her consciousness.

"Oman! Help me! Please!" She shot her plea out over and over, but Oman could not hear her cries.

Oman's forehead pressed against the tree, the forward motion of Dammerung developed enough pressure to crack a line across the skull. Pain was not an issue, but this prehistoric bone was the last vestige of his existence, if the only thing tethering him to reality broke, he would be gone in an instant, his second life now forfeit, only nothingness awaited. He laughed about his final thoughts before his coming end.

On his first departure from life he thought about his childhood, living in the darkest corners of a never ending slum, his rising to power through discovering his connection to the dead, his armies of corpses invading dozens of cities, his rule near complete.

Now in his second chance of last thoughts, the only thing he could think about was how good those things they called pancakes looked, and how sad he was of never getting a chance to try one.

He laughed with every crack of his housing.

He halted his maddened cackle when the cracks he heard were not coming from his skull. The space of time between the snaps became shorter and shorter. It became a reverse tug of war to see who would fall first between the acid chewed tree and the crumbling Necromancer.

Ceramic like shards pebbled off from Oman's eye sockets, one by one, three of his front teeth popped away, he heard what could have been a hundred rusted door hinges creak open at once, the colossal tree fell!

The pressure released. Dammerung placidly hopped onto the long tree going on its merry way, the forest grumbled as it saw its destined meal float away, the beads of light of Oman's eyes sparked a flash when he remembered the hero responsible for this feat.

"Familiar! Where are you?"

He saw the remains of ripped intestine and followed it to the hollowed cavity in the squirrel's belly. Blood Fucker was splayed out on the dirt face up, one leg twitching, eyes heavy barely showing a reflective glimmer of unlife in them.

"You've put a thousand years of a thousand familiars to shame with your repeated acts of bravery! Songs will be made of you for this! I will see to it myself! Come now, get up here so we may make our escape!"

Blood Fucker's seized to move, all the Eitherkreiss gone, he could hear the skull but his body could not respond.

Oman's fixed line of sight slowly lost view of the furry hero, "Get up you fool! Hurry! How dare you do this!? What will

I tell your master when she wakes up and doesn't see you? Don't you dare leave me with this troublesome duty! Curse you vermin, curse youuuuuuuuu!"

All he could do was scream, yet again now, just a passenger.

His self loathing was cut short by a new fresh hell, a cliff, a rather large, with a deep dark hole beneath it.

His last sight before engulfed in darkness was seeing a bridge the sword missed by only a few inches, then the void swallowed them all whole.

34

"Forest Fighting"

Ted felt like a passenger in his own body, he knew he wasn't dead, he felt his arms and legs busy doing something, probably violent, the moment reminded him of that one time his cousins stuffed him in a discarded cardboard box and pushed him down a steep hill.

He sensed the mighty thing in him driving his body to further harm, a series of blunt force shocks followed by what he deduced was dragon fire made him dread waking up to the pain waiting for him. When the stabbing sensations began he felt his blood leave his body.

Still he was glad he could contribute to the cause, even if it was just lending his body out like a busted up car to that thing within him. This was a good time as any to figure out who is this action star living for free in him.

"Um, hello? Excuse me, I know it's not a good time, but when you get a few seconds I'd like to have a chat with ya, cause you took over my body without my permission mind you, and yes I appreciate what your doing but I think you can see the violating implications of doing such a thing."

"Hey!" Said the entity, the word echoing around him, a voice so deep it rippled the plain of Ted's mindscape.

"Don't say it like that! That is not what this is, you are purposely making it sound weird and that's not cool." said an incorporeal voice.

"Who are you and why are you doing this?" Ted said.

"As you said, I'm a bit busy right now, could we do this some other time?"

"Yeah, yeah I know, I get it, sorry."

What felt like a flagpole was driven through Ted's shoulder.

"Ouch! What the actual fuck dude!?" Ted complained.

"Look!" the voice shouted so loud that Ted felt the pressure behind his eyes press so hard they could have popped out.

In the floating nothingness appeared a woman so large Ted was no bigger than the pupil in one of the giant's eyes.

Built of what looked like blue marble stood a titan of a woman, muscles thick and bulging, hard as ingots of iron, all wrapped in tattered leather from a dozen animals, a shield hung from her right arm, a metal warthog engulfed in flames decorated its center. An iron helmet hid her blue glowing eyes, what stood out the most from the already jaw dropping sight was the long braided beard that was embedded to the helmet in a decorative manner, covering the users face.

"Look little man, I'm busy...doing your job, so sit tight, shut up and I'll return the wheel to your pathetic body when I'm done or dead. And You're welcome by the way you ungrateful prick!" The barbarian giant yelled.

"First, that was super rude, second, at the very least tell me who you are." Ted said.

The warrior leaned in placing Ted between her two giant glowing eyes.

"I am YOUR purpose unfulfilled! I am the potential you rotted away! I am not just a Coalboar, I am THE COALBOAR! So stay quiet while I try and return some semblance of honor to our name, so would you kindly shut the hell up now?"

"Fine," Ted lowered his voice, "Big ass bearded bitch."

"What was that?"

"Nothing, nothing" Ted relented.

"That's what I thought, tiny redheaded bitch boy."

Despite the derogatory nature of the exchange, Ted felt some of his own pride survive the verbal spat. He was called a little bitch boy, but he took the insult from a phantom barbarian giant, in his book he still looked a little brave by the end of it.

The giant woman faded away to return to the battle at hand. Ted once again left in the vastness of his mind seeing how empty it was, he hoped this isn't proof of his hollow mind and possible idiocy.

He could not make up his mind on whether he should stay inside himself, or take command once more and face the horrors happening outside like a brave Coalboar.

He was protected from the outside battle, the adults were dealing with it. But being alone with his thoughts was not a fun thing at the moment either.

"Why does a giant woman live inside me? How long has she been in there? What has my family been hiding from me? Is Uli safe?"

Ted was surprised with himself that it had gone on this far, that despite the insanity of it all, and that there has been at least a dozen times that given the choice he would have left and called it a win he didn't. The answer for all this was Uli. He didn't want to see his friend get hurt, but there was always something extra, he could feel it whenever he wanted to run away, his feet somehow always made it into the shit show with Uli, was the Coalboar spirit to blame? Or was it him all along? As long as it kept him and Uli alive he was fine with either truth.

* * *

Carl was damp with dragonsack blood, the heat from the sigil burning his skin, he felt the power of Etheria flowing through him. He knew the words from the walking smoke machine were nothing more than lies. He repeated that truth to himself over and over again, the power in him was proof enough. But the seeds of doubt start small, perhaps true, perhaps false. But doubt finds fertile ground in imagination. As he said once before "What if?" is powerful and magically charged sentance, just speaking the two words together could bring great things, "What if the world was made of pizza, What if I asked out Debbie that one time, what If I had driven back home that night when I was super wasted?" It can work the blackest of magic as well, "What if I can get away with cheating on Debbie? What if the crazy guy full of smoke was telling the truth?"

All these thoughts are not good to juggle in one's mind in the middle of a battle. Especially when he was surrounded by the dragonsacks, that despite every solar flare of holy light leaving them extra crispy, they would breathe in the rotten magic around them and charge on.

Ted was in his very scary, but very useful berserker murder mode, cutting the dragon mimics in two with nothing but a small camping knife, but they never stopped getting back together to continue the attack.

The real pain in their collective ass was the fake ranger now turned into a smoke spewing abomination with blond highlights. Lighting quick and capable of producing an infinite amount of weapons out of that odd smoke, Swords, hammers, phallic looking clubs, which the fake ranger stroked a few times like a teen on a home alone Friday night.

Mr. Sundae was on his way to Uli and the sword, thankfully Ted would cut his path, throwing him back into the tiny skirmish.

It was becoming apparent to Carl that this was not a fight they could win, but they could at least stall them enough to give Uli enough time to wake up and even maybe reach Aiden's final resting place.

He felt a hard crack on his chest, a sizable chunk of the sigil broke off dropping to the bottom of his properly tucked in shirt. The flashlight's holy glow dimmed slightly. The dragonsack saw this as an opportunity to strike, Carl aimed the light onto them, not as powerful as before it still hit them like boiling water.

"Looks like your cereal box prize is running out of batteries there kid," Mr. Sundae scoffed while elegantly dodging every one of Ted's attacks.

"Sooner or later you and your little buddy here are going to run out of strength, I got all the time in Thira boys, do you?"

Mr. Sundae wasn't wrong, but he was bluffing, running his powers at full overdrive longer than he's had to for centuries, and he was down to his last two magic cigarettes.

A screech from one of the bigger dragonsack's drew the demigod's attention. The larger than most monster was now impaled by three spear thin black branches, the forest joined in with the dragon sack for a good scream, but with its own rendition of a roar of satisfaction. The forest found Uli to be a rather annoying meal to catch, and opted to brave it out and go for some magical sustenance from the other formidable foes in its presence.

The distraction gave Ted the instance he needed for a nightstick powered blow on Mr. Sundae, shooting him ten feet across the battle.

The forest itself was reaching to Carl's chest, he broke away the first row of branches but was burned by a stream of fire from one of the newly regenerated dragonsacks.

The impaled dragon hybrid fought back, thrashing around trying to push its way of his impalement, the branch was sucking its blood into the crack of the bark.

The hybrid began to thin, its rapid loss of mass was macabre to witness. As if an industrial vacuum was placed to maximum output.

All present took warning that a third party had joined the battle, and it was driven by a simple yet powerful need, hunger.

The forest closed in, branches, roots, even the dead pine thorns scattered around encroaching on anything with a pulse.

Mr. Sundae looked on at the havoc the forest would bring forth, slow going, but coming from every direction, one cannot keep eyes in so many directions.

He saw a perfect opening to where Dammerung and Uli had escaped. He shot up and flashed his way to the unchecked gap, he was hard to catch but yet again thwarted, the hydraulic press of Ted's arms bear hugging him.

Fire enveloped the whole location, the dragonsack platoon went into a panic, launching their rancid fires in every direction.

The once peaceful campfire had turned into a hellscape even more disturbing than the already horrid forest aesthetic. The sight was visceral and bloody, just like the battles taken place there in the days of old.

The forgotten forest celebrated that its once silent stillness was filled with the screams and blood of warriors, and that it could drink all of the life out of them was an added plus.

"You're fast for a big boy," Mr. Sundae head butted Ted's stone face. The blows struck true, the full force of a demigod landing with brutal force, disfiguring Ted's nose and splitting his lip, Ted never screamed once, his only reaction was tightening his spine breaking grip.

The Coalboar spirit was not infinite in strength or control of Ted, the prolonged bout and repeated strikes to the head finally did some damage to the tank of a man.

"What the hell is happening, ouch! My nose?! Not again!" Ted, the true Ted, came into control of his body and saw Mr. Sundae rather a bit too inside his personal space.

"Oh shit!" Ted said, Mr. Sundae smiled, Ted's strength was no longer superhuman.

Mr. Sundae loaded and fired a final headbutt. Ted's barbaric passenger within came forth once more and countered the headbutt with his own.

"Dammit with you," Mr. Sundae barked. Ted put all his strength into the bear hug, the pressure was such that a prehistoric animal would beg for mercy. Mr. Sundae felt his mortal body react, not an expert in human anatomy, he could at least understand that hearing things pop inside you was not good.

The demonic tree roots found them convenient prey and wrapped around them, pulling them down to the floor to further wrap them in a spiderweb of sticks

"Oh gees, heeeeeelp! true Ted yelled.

"Don't let him go Ted, for Uli's sake don't let him go!" Carl said, his holy light now blinking, his relic necklace now down only to the size of a small rock. The stalling was done, the battle was over. His words of assistance only meant to give Ted the final push of bravery before they were all swallowed. Carl found a warrior's peace in the idea that the battle was not lost to the enemy at hand, but by the forest. They bought Uli some time, but her fate was perhaps as sealed as theirs.

***

"Let go of me you overgrown prick," Mr. Sundae felt Ted's industrial strength kung fu grip fluctuate at an irregular rhythm, every time he felt he could get loose, the pressure would trigger again.

The branches around them did not help the matter.

Both Mr. Sundae and Ted could feel the branches stick into them, "Is this how you wanna go kid? Getting the worst suck job in your life?"

That disgusting statement fell on deaf ears, the cycling with Ted's inner warrior was becoming erratic by the second, making the easily woozy Ted dizzy enough to throw up right onto Mr. Sundae's face.

The demigod had partaken in the most hedonistic of parties with gods and humans alike, indulged in sickening depravity. Never did he ever think that he would one day be wrapped in the world's most disturbing wicker basket, being hugged by a mortal who just decorated his face with tomato soup mixed with sandwich shrapnel. He thought of his now gone brothers and fathers and how they would laugh at his current plight, oh how the mighty have fallen indeed.

Following the up chucking, Ted fainted, the trees now fully stabbing them, Ted's grip was gone but the wrapped branches made any effort to escape futile.

His essence now being drained, he so wanted to have one final smoke. He was about to experience what only a small number of immortals have had the chance to feel, death.

Ted was stuck in his mindscape when he saw the giant Coalboar progenitor shrink by the second.

"We're dying aren't we?" Ted said.

"Pretty much yeah." answered the original Coalboar.

"I wonder if Uli woke up and made it out."

"Hell if I know."

"No news is good news I guess."

"Yeah, I guess it is."

"So, am I still a disgrace to the bloodline?" Ted asked.

The marble barbarian pondered, now only half her size but still towering over tiny Ted.

"Perhaps you are Ted."

He took the damning statement with a calm defeated grace, sadness still apparent on his now translucent face.

"But perhaps, not as big a disappointment as we elders thought."

"I'll take it," being proclaimed only a mild disappointment was as far as Ted was concerned a win. The unknown of Uli's location still weighed heavy on him.

* * *

Carl was in the process of offing the same dragonsack for what felt like the eleventh time. The fiery glow of the emblem of Etheria being nothing more but a defective night light.

The dragosacks around him had lost interest in him, focusing more on their own survival from the unrelenting blood forest. One or two of the hybrids managed to escape. Others while fleeing fell victim to the branches hiding in the thick darkness surrounding them, it was an absorbing stalemate at times between the forest and the kind of sort of dragons. There was simply too much forest to contend with.

Carl may have gotten one demonic monkey off his back, but the fact that both he and Ted were next on the menu was an absolute.

They needed something big, something massive, they needed a miracle. Carl had seen many of those in the last twenty four hours, but none of them fell into absolute miracle territory. He needed something the church of Etheria would build a holiday around.

His power dwindling, all was lost, nothing left, he yanked out the sigil from his blood drenched shirt, wrapped around his trusty taser and began to prey.

"Etheria, your humble servant, my time has come but I wish not to perish for nothing, please with the last of your might, help me ignite this for one last time!"

He gripped the taser tight and hoped against hope that she would listen to one final prayer.

He raised the less lethal weapon and pressed it on, waiting for his miracle.

None came, all that was seen and heard was the iconic yet lackluster zap of the taser.

Perhaps the sigil has done all it can do. Perhaps his time had come and could go no further despite his reignited dream.

Perhaps the smoke man was right and that was all that was left of Etheria.

No one left to pray or hope to. But in the end, he was most hurt by the fact that he most likely would have disappointed his father.

"I'm sorry Dad, I wish I could have gone a bit longer."

The small nub that was left of the symbol glowed once more. Carl looked in wonder. "Dad?" He asked, the amulet answered with a small pulse of light, "Dad!"

It wasn't Etheria who was protecting him. What made that necklace powerful was not the love and faith he had with the sun goddess, it was the love and faith of the first to protect him, to love him, to teach him about being a good man. No holy book, religion or church needed, It was Dad!

Tears rolled down his eyes knowing now what he should have known all along, but the moment was much too short.

"I wish to go on longer Pop, but I need one more miracle, I need to help my friends, I need to complete my quest."

The nub shined in response, growing brighter and brighter

to blinding luminous capacity.

"Thanks Pop, love you."

He wiped the tears away and wrapped the necklace around the taser once more, he raised it to the heavens, the radiance of the necklace engulfed the taser, its power ran down into Carl, his body lit up like a life form composed of pure light.

He switched the taser on, what came forth was not its startling spark and buzz, what exploded out was thunderous lighting, the sky lit ablaze as the bolt reached the clouds, the thunder cracked loud enough to awaken people in the far off towns, lighting danced around the battlefield faster than the eye could follow, a single blade of lighting blasted into the forest. It crashed around hitting tree and dragon alike, the dragonsacks would burst like frogs in a microwave, trees exploded into towers of fire, burning hotter than a plasma furnace, the forest ripped out an agonizing wail worthy of a thousand banshees.

The light coming from the attack grew so ferociously abrasive it rivaled staring at the sun. All was swallowed by light, taser shaking in his hand at sonic speed, the amulet crumbling to dust.

"Goodbye Dad."

All Carl could do was smile, he did not know what would come next, but he got his miracle in the end and even better, it came from his father.

The dancing storm swallowed the campsite battle whole, a pillar of light as tall as a skyscraper raged on, as if the finger of Etheria herself landed on Thira to usher the end of days.

All was consumed and burned, the scorched earth concept

was taken to maximum prejudice.

Carl had been reminded that his dear old Dad was known to always overdo it, be it with holiday decorations or burnt burgers.

Tonight he was making sure everybody was well done, apparently including Carl and Ted.

The pillar disappeared in an instant, all that was left was charbroiled earth.

35

"And Then There Were Three-ish"

Oman laid on the left side of his skull, looking at Uli's broken body, she breathed still but barely.

He had no clue on what to do next, the thought of being stuck there for eternity looking at Uli rot away as an army of souls ate her sanity was a fate worse than the many hells he explored in his youth.

Earlier a blast of energy was felt behind him, the cavernous quake rumbled and he feared an avalanche of rock would further ruin his already shitty circumstances. He deduced that Carl and Ted had made their last stand, even the little squirrel did his part.

He looked around where he could, piecing together this had been some moat of sorts long ago, made to safeguard something, probably the final resting place of Prince Aiden.

Oman's despair spiral was interrupted by the wet impact of what sounded like a two hundred pound tomato landing on concrete.

"Gods, what now?" He muttered.

"AND THEN THERE WERE THREE-ISH"

A charred dragonsack coughed out a dry scream, its lungs nothing more but sandpaper.

The wet slap of its humanoid feet approached. Heavily injured, just barely evading heavenly justice.

Hungry and hurt, one eyeball hanging, its head flailing about, neck broken from the fall, its intestines dragging behind it from the concussive force of the fall.

With its one good eye, it saw two food sources with every sway of his penduling head. Uli emanated rotted magic, tastes awful but good in a pinch.

Oman knew its intent and did the only thing he could, scream. It served well enough to get the dragonsack's attention, it toppled onto its knees to collect Oman, its boney fingers gripping him, salivating for salvation.

"Go on you disgusting lizard! I hope my Eitherkreiss rots your insides and serves you with only endless bouts of shit!"

The dragon hybrid knew not what the silly skull said, it opened its mouth sucking in Oman's dwindling life force, the dragonsack organs and bones shifting into place and reconstituting itself.

"How do I taste? My thoughts!? The memories of my powers!" Oman continued,"You're half dead, it was ill conceived of you to grab a Necromancer, you probably knock your prey unconscious before the feed, hard to konk out a skull."

The stream of Eitherkreiss pumping into the beast stopped mid current, leaving the dragonsack in a state of confusion, its body felt heavy, it now had to force and push the magic food into himself.

Oman's evil cackle burst out, every evil guffaw oozing his not forgotten villainous past. He questioned if doing evil unto evil still constitutes evil?

He relented on the conundrum, why ruin a good moment with overthinking?

"My turn," Oman opened his pearly white jaw and pulled back his stolen magic, with interest. The dragon felt as if Oman was not only taking back his arcane life force, but taking the dragon's mind for his own.

"Not used to your victim fighting back demon? You take and take, but you never thought it worked both ways, don't look so angry, I am not stealing, I am simply borrowing, absolutely everything."

The dragon's body went still, silent and statuesque, it wanted to howl, scream in terror but no such thing happened, Its arm refusing to move by his command.

"Ah wonderful, for a moment there I did not think it would work, you have no idea how good it feels to have a limb or two of my own once more."

36

"House Party"

Carl was halfway through the bridge, Ted's arm over his shoulder, he had the luck of collecting Blood Fucker's remains on his way from the decimated campsite.

He had wrapped Blood Fucker's entrails around Ted's neck. Carl was a super nice guy, but he couldn't do everything.

Did I mention they were both stark naked? Carl's wonderful Dad did a splendid job with his over the top orbital strike beam, eradicating all evil, turns out the heavenly death ray doesn't hurt the righteous, but it still burns clothing away.

Carl used the blinding light show to pick up Ted and get them out of there in Uli's direction.

They were hours away from daylight, Carl saw the bridge Dammerung failed to take over the pit.

Logic dictated to Carl that Uli and company took the bridge, but logic hadn't checked with the party for a while now.

The cold night air was easily felt by Ted and Carl, the adrenaline of the night's events slowly fading, the fact they were alive was a blessing, but they were a few degrees away from hypothermia.

The other side of the bridge was far, Carl heard a noise behind him, one similar to that of a science fiction ray gun shooting at an alien. When he looked behind, the fading flair of a laser beam pittered away.

One of those dragons was shooting at them from the bottom of the pit, "One of them must have escaped! The moron fell down there."

A second beam missed but managed to graze one side of the bridge.

More and more tiny beams shot up, each one nearly aimed with the intent of cutting down the bridge.

"We gotta move man! Move, move!" Carl commanded.

They wobbled at a hurried pace to the end of the bridge, moving with only the most moderate of acceleration, looking more like an old couple doing their morning jog.

The end of the bridge was visible at the very least, with no sign of foes or Uli for that matter, they dared not look behind them, they knew what could happen, and sometimes ignorance and uncertainty are a good combination for escape tactics.

It's a good thing they didn't look back at the moment, because both support ropes on the bridge were very much on fire. They could hear how the heat of the flames snapped the fibers of the very sturdy but very ancient bridge.

"Come on, just a little more Ted," Carl was developing a rather nasty habit of white lies, but fake carrots got the mule to move, and move they had to.

Both ropes snapped simultaneously, the belly pulling gravity drop hit Ted and Carl with a delayed effect.

Ted grabbed a plank with one good arm, Carl managed to grip with both hands, they huffed and puffed as they got their bearings.

"Ted, don't move!"

"Why? Why not? What happened, what do you see?"

"Your penis is way too close to my face man?"

Ted looked down and saw Carl too close for comfort to his manly danglers.

"Oh crap dude, I'm sorry."

"It's fine, not your fault, let's gently climb up."

"Right."

From the bottom of the collapsed bridge something made its way up the bridge turned ladder.

The shaking sway of the climb gave some appendages a bit of centrifugal momentum causing Ted's member to slap Carl in the face with enough force to understand what parts of said member made contact with his left cheek and eye.

The Church of Etheria has antiquated concepts of the love between two people of the same gender. Carl felt that Etheria would have no issue with two people of proper age responsibly loving each other, no matter the sex.

He had once or twice wondered if he had such inclinations, but coming face to face with Ted's manhood made it all at once clear that some man on man action was not on his radar.

"Ted, for the love of Etheria, start climbing!"

"Oh yeah, right, right, sorry, sorry but, so sorry."

"Move dammit!"

Ted used his faulty arm to hoist himself up, whatever was climbing up was doing it in an uneven pattern.

At first view Carl saw a dragonsack with a broken neck,

its head wiggling around with every grip of a plank. It was carrying something over its shoulder.

They dared not look back, Ted made it over the ledge, falling unceremoniously on the hard stony floor right on his injured shoulder letting out an excruciating yell.

He helped Carl over, now self-conscious of keeping anything below his non-existent belt at a polite distance.

"The second it peaks its head we start kicking it like crazy!" Carl ordered.

"Good idea!" Ted said. It was the only thing they could do without weapons while being buck naked.

They heard the creature make it to the edge, claws grabbing hold of the final plank.

They rushed to the edge conjuring up whatever strength they had left, unleashing a flurry of stomps and kicks.

They yelled with exhausted rage, not at all looking forward to another contentious round with the near immortal monsters.

"Stop that you imbeciles! You'll knock us down!"

Carl stopped immediately, Ted put in a couple of good kicks before Carl yanked him away.

"Oman!?" Carl asked, panting like a winded dog.

They cautiously looked over the edge of the ledge to find very much a dragonsack with a broken neck, sword strapped to its back by Carl's belt, and Uli over its shoulder, but Oman was nowhere to be seen.

"Oman, where are you? What the hell is this?"

"Help us you nitwits!"

They hesitated to grab the Burnt claws of the hybrid mutant, but eventually helped Oman up. Ted placed Uli down, Carl rested the Dammerung on the rocky floor.

They got a good view of where Oman's voice was coming from, his head was lodged in a large cavity where the creature's guts should have been.

"You finally got your own body Oman."

"Yes, yes, but where are your clothes?"

"A blast of holy light burned them off."

"Ah yes, naturally," Oman said, "I agree this thing is a less than optimal substitute for my original form, burnt and broken, but easy to drive non the less."

He walked towards them with the grace of a glitched automaton. The spectacle of his movement was ugly to look at, the swaying head due to a broken neck was especially disturbing.

"We found B.F. looking like this, care to elaborate?" Carl asked.

"He proved his worth as a familiar, he did everything he could to save his master and he did so bravely." Oman said with a somber histrionic tone.

"Can he be brought back?" Ted asked, "I heard you can only do it once."

"Familiars work differently, it's not a soul per se, it is a netherbeing taking over a body, much like how I did this creature here, if the original corpse can still function, its master can reconstitute them. It has to be done quickly, if not the nether creature's tether to the body fades. He needs Uli."

They looked at Uli, battered and beaten but for the most part no worse for the ware.

"She's stuck in a battle for control of her body, the whole forest came into contact with her."

"Wake her up, we got shit to do and get the hell out of here,"

Ted said.

"Easier said than done, her mind is an ocean at the moment and she cannot find a shore, someone has to go into her."

"Inside her?" Ted asked.

"Ted, not now." Carl said.

"Okay."

"Now that I can actually help, I can assist in infiltrating her mind, locate her and help her to wake up. We must make haste." Oman knelt over Uli's head, her face grimaced and ached as if electrocuted.

"Why are you still here Oman?" Ted asked, "Once you got a body you could have left us all to rot and go off and rule the world and stuff."

Oman took a moment to answer, his ember lit eyes looking at the two nude men.

"I was going to," Oman looked away, "But we have a quest to complete, and I can't have Volshtadt be present if I am going to take back this world which is rightfully mine. So don't believe this was an act of friendship."

"Oh we would never," Carl said smiling.

"Good, good, now Theodore, you know her the most, best you go."

"Will it hurt?" Ted asked.

"Ted!" yelled Carl, his bullshit defense thoroughly depleted.

"Okay yeah, sorry, what do I have to do?"

"Lay next to her I will help you dive into her psyche"

"And then?"

"Find her, help her regain control over her mind. Uli is drowning in an miasma of souls, their memories of combat and sorrow ripping her sanity apart, she needs a memory, a strong one, an important one. One that can serve as a beacon back to the waking world. A shared memory so powerful that it eradicates all other presence within her. Do you have a memory like that?"

Ted stared at the soon dawning sky. The cold of the night giving its final attack before the warmth of sunlight scares it off. He went still, eyes going wide with the realization of what that memory had to be.

"Yeah, I got one."

Ted laid next to Uli, he looked at her struggling face, She was alive but in a living hell. She needed him more than ever, and he was going to do everything he could to help.

"How is this supposed to go down?"

Oman did not give any explanation, he poked a drop of blood from a wound that was in abundant supply on both of them and placed it on each of their foreheads.

His eyes went a glow, jaw going up and down at an alarming velocity, he ended the jittering with *"Haltram."*

Ted fell instantly asleep, driven into a darkness much like when he was with his ancestor.

"I can't see a damn thing."

He saw in the distance what looked like a wave pushing to him. A wave made of horses, knights, blood, fire and pain, all of it rolling and collapsing on itself.

He brought his arms up and braced for impact. It crashed on him, feeling the full weight of it, the stench of war impacted him as hard as his body felt getting hit by a whole army. The sweat, blood, bodies and blades, swallowing him into the undertow of war.

"Keep your head about you boy! Ignore the lunacy around you." Oman's bodiless voice echoed into the ocean of war.

Ted swam up from the orgy of combat and managed to step

on top of it like solid ground, it swayed and fluxed, making it hard to keep his balance.

"Find her Ted!" Oman said.

"How? It's a fucking shit show!" he ran around and saw a tower at the middle of the field, warriors and wizards climbing up trying to reach Uli, no doors or windows, any who tried to reach the top Uli would knock out.

"Uli!"

"Ted?!"

"Uli we have to get out of here!"

"What? I can't hear you!"

Ted made his way through,"How come they don't attack me?"

"You're invisible to them, they're frenzy focused on the battle, but it won't last for long," Oman said, "She can't hear you Ted, you have to get close.

"Uli! You gotta hear me! I'm trying to get you out of here."

"Uli, do you remember that one time six years ago? Freddy Norby's house party, at his cabin!"

The battlefield phased away to a house party, teenagers lost in alcoholic glee. The cabin that was more of a mansion/fortress had its expensive sound system blaring the demonic gunk teenagers of said era would call music.

Everybody was there, jocks, theater geeks, the alternative club, all were welcome to Freddy's place, loved by all and friend to everybody. Of average height, silver blond hair, thin of build and silver eyes. If he had sported long pointy ears, he would be the spitting image of a high elf. His family was well off and well aware of the party, the wealthiest family in the countryside, they knew these ragers would help their son in the future, connections made, friendships solidified, and if anybody did something stupid while under the influence, blackmail is a useful tool when the time came.

The party was roaring, both the battle and the cabin party playing over each other, like television channels mixing in the feed. Neither scene of chaos interacting, the only mingling was that of the crazed noise of combat and the top forty mix fighting for sonic dominance.

In the middle of the chaos, the past selves of Uli and Ted stood, younger, both with less body hair or curves, no one at the party paying attention to them, both drinking cheap beer as if it was water.

"We were drinking like fish, neither of us were big drinkers but we figured we should celebrate since it was my last year in school, we were waxing poetic on what we were going to do in the future." Ted narrated.

Throughout the whole night young Ted could not stop locking eyes with a stuffed boar, perfectly preserved, its fur pristine, its eyes masterfully maintained to keep a moist hydrated look.

One beer after another, Ted could not understand why he kept looking at it.

"After your fifth beer you went to pee, there was a line at the bathroom, too long, you got scared of just peeing your pants then and there, ever the resourceful one you are you figured you could just do your business outside."

Uli, stealthy, made her way out through the sliding door to the back. She sneaked into the vast dark woods, eager to relieve her bladder that was full to bursting of the cheapest beer that one rich kid could get.

She popped a squat behind a small pile of fallen trees, halfway through relieving herself she could hear the distant laughter of teenagers, she hid her head emulating a turtle. Uli feared that she had been found in such a precarious position and would be subject to the humiliation expected from teenage boys. She quickly scanned around the location and found no witnesses watching her call to nature.

She zipped up and went to investigate the source of the joking and mockery, tiptoeing from one tree to another as not to be seen.

The closer she got to the laughter and adolescent banter, she could hear a constant rustling of fallen foliage, the repetitive motion of raking leaves on your front lawn came to her mind, or two men wrestling on a mound of dead maple leafs.

"Go Ted go! Go Ted go! Get it!" said one of the inebriated teens. She accelerated her approach and found cover behind a mossy overgrowth, and at last saw what had the boys in such jolly elation.

Five idiots surrounded Ted, on his knees fully nude, the taxidermied wild boar in front of him, his actions with said wild pig does not require heavy detail, I will only report that he was "giving it to her" with the drive of a possessed animal in heat.

Ted's eyes were whited out, controlled by an unseen force.

"I always acted like I blacked out that day. I didn't know what was happening, I wasn't driving my body but it still didn't feel right."

Long ago, the Coalboar clan would partake in sexual congress with forest guardians disguised as boars as to gain their favor and power, because gods find it far more hilarious to make humans bed zoo animals for some reason, many a regular boar would be taken by accident in such activities, but the Coalboars would say otherwise.

Entranced, Ted saw Uli hiding in the brush snapping him out of it. When he fully came to and got his bearings, he saw the laughing jocks, the forest, the taxidermied animal still attached to him. No cup of coffee would have awoken him faster than the realization of what he was stuck in the middle of.

He screamed for only a moment and fell silent, his cry of horror cut short by his stomach deciding it was time to throw up the copious quantities of alcohol he had ingested that evening. The roar of laughter by the small crowd inevitably followed.

"Shit Coalboar! You are gonna be a legend in town forever!" said one of the drunks, "You'll never live this down bro! You're gonna have to leave town dude!"

Uli leapt out of hiding to aid Ted, placing her oversized jacket over her naked friend.

"You guys are sick, leave him alone!" but none paid attention.

"He was just drunk, leave him be," Ted remained catatonic.

"Come on Ted, let's get out of here."

"I, I'm stuck."

"Shit, really?" the five watchers shot their beer out of their noses.

"Like a dog! Like a damned dog!"

"I knew you Coalboars were backwater, I didn't know just how much!"

Uli and Ted knew this is not the thing that will die off, this will follow Ted for life.

"At that moment you made a decision," older Ted said as he watched a memory he wished he could very much forget.

Young Uli grabbed the crying young Ted and saw the resignation in his face.

"I am going to make them forget." Young Uli said.

"How?"

"And then you did it," said older Ted

"You have to make a promise, an oath, but it demands a promise to be fulfilled to seal it. Do you promise?" asked young Uli, Ted didn't think twice.

"Yeah, yeah, yes I promise!"

"Errfasen."

The leaves around the drunk teens gripped on their tattered sneakers, none of them having ever seen magic before, some of them just drunkenly surprised.

"And Uli can do magic? Oh you two are perfect for each other, the witch and the freak!" yelled the ringleader.

"That's when you and I made the pact of Ozen Maloique."

Uli long ago found a grimoire of Ozen Maloique, a multi branch wizard who saw how to combine different schools of magic by finding the connecting points in each system.

Psychic magic and necromancy meet many times in the Venn diagram of spell casting. This is where Ozen developed the memory killer spell. Killing a memory is serious business, most taboo for the problematic implications of mind invasion alone.

Magic was now illegal, mind magic was on a different level of no no's all together.

Such a powerful spell had two downsides. The magical rebound can kill the caster. The second is the trade off necessary to perform the contract, a memory for a memory.

Five drunk teens would have to be five of Uli's memories, and not just random ones like grocery shopping, or returning a movie to the rental store. It had to be good ones, the best ones. Uli knew which to use, not hesitating in putting them on the magical chopping block.

She pulled her replica ceremonial dagger out and placed a cut over her right eyebrow.

"What are you doing? Don't kill them, Uli, it's not worth it."

"No you idiot, close your eyes." Ted did and she cut his eyebrow as well, mirroring hers.

"Ouch!" he sniffled.

Ozen had a thing for blood from around the eyes, under the school of thought it had a special effect on memory spells. She stretched out her right arm, her hand spreading its five fingers aiming them at the jerks.

"A pact made and a promise signed, death of a memory shall be paid in kind."

The bullies mocked her words and her dramatic pose, threatening to call the police if she didn't stop her illegal ritual.

"By the words of the mind mage, your memory fades, by the claim of the name, I call you now Ozen Maloique!"

The black ooze of necromancy cascaded out of Uli's mouth by the gallon. The thick tar arose and took the shape of a robed figure, from it a skull with several ocular cavities peered out onto its victims. Ozen Maloique had come, and he demanded payment.

"Choose your thoughts to pay," he whispered.

Uli answered immediately.

-Her first and only kiss with Ted, it was magical, but not for the obvious reason a million love stories like to sing about. They had known each other for so long, people talked, they talked, it felt natural for these two to at some point to fall into the what many say would have been the natural way of things, chemistry, connection, kinship what have you, but when they locked eyes and then their lips, the sparks that flew were not of two lovebirds, their was actually no sparks at all, halfway through it they both started to laugh, the alien sensation was so awkwardly comical that instead of destroying what they had, it proved that they didn't need it, they were together for every other reason then that. Love like those seen on the cover of drug store paperback novels burned up faster than a cheap cigarette, they knew they were besties in it for the long run, never again burdened by the wonderful yet heavy shackles of a love that could fizzle out.

-Next on the chopping block was when she told her parents she could perform magic, not only that, but that she wanted to develop it as much as she could. Her parents loved her dearly, but she dreaded that the idea of their little girl practicing forbidden arts, the idea of confession gave Uli terror at the backlash this would have in their family. When she gathered the courage to announce to them that "She wants to control the dead," Mama and Papa Einsworth simultaneously took two deep breaths, looked at her dead serious and said, "But you can still be our daughter, right?"

"HOUSE PARTY"

-Her first spell, she brought an ant back to life. No spell book to read from, no wand or blood sacrifice, she just really wanted that little guy to make it back to his ant hill. It took her a hundred tries but she did it.

The tiny insect exploded three seconds after the spell was completed, but it still counted.

- Next was that on time she beat DURIN'S SPACE ADVENTURE! An already old eight-bit video game that she could not get past the first level for the most of her childhood. It wasn't till a drunken all-nighter with Ted that she made it to the final boss and defeated him, nothing up to that moment had given her the sense of triumph that the ending screen of that game gave her. You may scoff at this, but only those who have been destroyed for days on end by a digital depiction of a vampire or armored pig understand the sense of elation and vindication that only comes from thwarting a programmed depiction of evil that had slayed your ass time and time again.

Then came the final memory, it had to be a real good one, the type that anchors the rest of who you are to what you will become, Uli had to end the choices with a bang, and she had a real doozy for the gloopy dead guy before her.

-The first time Ted invited her to play with him. How that millisecond made the foundation for a lifelong friendship. After the forfeit of a moment, her only recollection of it was through Ted himself, he knew she gave it away for him, so he made it a mission to make sure she could have at least a reported memory of that fateful day.

"I find the payment suitable," Ozen Maloique said. He faced

the drunks and whispered *"Eninnerung."*

A black light shot out of the skeleton mage, five beams right through all their foreheads.

All five drunks fell to the floor, their memories of the night burnt out of them, something that could be easily blamed on the less than fine beer.

Uli fell with them to the floor, convulsing, tar seeping out of her.

Ted managed to release himself from the dried out boar and checked on Uli.

"I cleaned the magic gunk off of you and took you to the hospital, they attributed it all to alcohol poisoning since you did have enough to drink that night too. On that night you sacrificed five memories for me, memories that formed you, parts that made you YOU. When you woke up I could tell, it was still you, just missing something. At the hospital we remembered the promise, you said you would never use it but I insisted that you should."

The blood drenched warriors around them froze.

"You Coalboars, strange bastards aren't ya?"

Ted turned to see Adult Uli standing next to the now double stuffed animal.

He ran to hug her, "Yup, that's why we hang out with wizards, religious mall cops and talking skulls."

The frozen warriors turned to ash, blown away into the night sky. The reunited duo began to fade from the memory as well.

"We got a quest to finish," Ted said with actual non ironic enthusiasm, stunning Uli to smile.

"Damn right we do," she said, "Hey was it fun to see an old flame of yours, you know, the pig"

"Oh just shut up."

Ted gave one last look at the dead and dried creature, he blushed, feeling the ache one would only feel for the one that got away. Though said in jest, he was painfully reminded that his bloodline was very much backwater barbarian pervy hillbillies.

Uli and Ted opened their eyes to the now sun drenched sky of the living, Oman still deep in meditation over them, Carl to their side, hands clenched to one another mumbling deep in prayer. Uli and Ted looked at each other and shared a quiet smile before the rest saw them finally awake.

Uli looked down at Ted and did a double take of Carl.

"Hey, why are you two butt ass naked?"

37

"Unrest In Peace"

Oman's borrowed body crumbled to pieces like burnt charcoal, His skull rolling out of its short lived home, "Drat, it was nice to have extremities again, if only for a moment."

Sadness projected with every syllable.

Uli really did like the group hug she got once fully awake, but reminded the two men they were still in full doodly bits mode at the moment, they jumped away from her in embarrassment, both cupping their not so private privates. She had a good laugh from the sight, in the privacy of her now non-invaded mind she didn't mind all that much being the ham in a rather nice naked sandwich.

"Well done giant, you brought her back," Oman said from his view from the bottom, never the prude but was not at all pleased with his view of Ted and Carl. "Would someone please place me somewhere else, the view here is most horrid." the yet again bodiless skull requested.

Uli asked about Blood Fucker, when she didn't see or feel her nimble little friend running in joy around her she feared the worst. He was neatly placed a dozen feet away, with his insides placed next to him rolled up as one would a water hose.

She ran and knelt next to him. "Oh my poor baby, my poor beautiful baby, what happened to you?"

Oman told her of Blood Fucker's heroic last stand, tears welling in her eyes, amazed of how far the little one would and could go to save her.

She found her ceremonial dagger, pricked her finger and let the blood fall into the squirrel's mouth. She rummaged her bag for her spell book and located the section on familiars.

She drew in the loose gravel a circle around Blood Fucker's small body. She closed her eyes, trying to tap into the Either, the once difficult to access space was now smoother than a sliding door, she saw Blood Fucker's essence floating above his remains. She hovered one hand over him, gravel shaking away from the circle the closer her hand got. If Oman had lips he would have smiled.

"Your time is not yet set, your mission not completed, return at once and never be defeated! *ZURUCK!*"

Blood Fucker's body bounced from the floor in a series of spasms, much the same you see from a dead patient being shocked back to life. By the third shock of the invisible jumper cables of magic, his guts rolling back into his belly like a snappy measuring tape, Blood Fucker popped up on his hind feet, wasting no time to jump on Uli and cover her in absolutely awful smelling kisses, "My wonderful little shit, my brave little squirrel!" she cradled him like a wee babe,"Oman told me all about it, how you saved me, him and the sword."

The warmth of the moment was put on hold, all eyes widening in panic.

"The sword!" Uli said.

"Sword!" Ted Said.

"Dammerung!" Oman said.

"Squeak, squeak!" you know who said that.

On top of not knowing where the sword was, it was not until now that they got a good look at the location they were at.

A large mesa with a long deep moat all around it, keeping the forest well away from its reach, the boulders and stones all varying tones of orange and red.

"Where did it go? It was right there!" The gravel around Dammerung's original placing showed its outline, just no blade.

"It couldn't have gotten up and left, not without B.F. or Oman."

"Wait, I feel something," Uli said, hushing them up instantly, "Can you guys? Like a buzz."

"By Ornak's fire this place is dripping with it," Oman said.

"You two magic folks care to fill us in," Carl said, still holding his manhood out of sight.

Uli took her satchel and jacket off, giving them to Ted and Carl to cover up what they could. Carl had put on his utility belt on his nude form but did not like the exotic dancing implications.

"This place is emanating holy magic out of the butt, Dammerung must have tapped into it. Cover up your tools boys, we are going sword hunting." Uli said, getting one last gander.

Small help the bag and jacket were to cover their manhood, but it was enough for them to feel some level of decorum restored.

They ran off in separate directions, Uli holding Oman, B.F following closely behind. They went on, paying close attention to hopefully hear the wind chimes of the sword that drove them all mad during the trip.

"You haven't noticed, have you?" Oman asked.

"Oh I knew Ted had that birthmark, but man Carl, like wow, good for him."

"No! You did a resurrection spell."

"So?"

"Plus you felt the holy Eitherkreiss all around." Oman said.

"Well it's so much, really hard not to notice."

"Before you could barely notice my silly apprentice, and you did not suffer any rebound after the ritual either."

"Holy crap you're right! How?"

"It was from contact with the forest, you took in so much rotted Eitherkreiss, it almost killed you, now that you purged a great deal of it, you are still overcharged."

"Small blessings huh."

"Don't say that, you'll start sounding like the acolyte, you are lucky though, since you're going to perform the resurrection by yourself."

Uli stopped her trot and turned Oman to look at her, "You can't be serious."

"I don't make jokes often girl, and this isn't one of them. I used up my own reserves to allow Ted to infiltrate your mind to wake you up, what I have left is to barely exist on this plain of reality."

"I can bring back Blood Fucker sure, but not Aiden, that's a whole other ball game." Uli said.

"It is our only choice, before any more denizens of Volshtadt come to stop us."

"But…"

"Apprentice!" Oman scolded, "You are no chosen one, nor touched by the gods, or blessed by a shaman. You have something better."

"My can do attitude?"

"Gods no. You are not chosen or anointed into purpose, you developed this lunatic idea and are seeing it through, knowing full well you could stop at any time. You are not chosen, you chose, and that overrides any need for those cumbersome things such as fate, you must choose one more time, to do this, not because you have to, but because you want to, and you can."

"Why are you being so nice to me, weren't you like trying to take over the world and stuff?"

"I know, I hate it so much, it seems the company you keep does affect you, meaning you all are contagious, and I despise you for infecting me."

"Guys! Uli!!" Carl ran up behind them keeping the satchel firmly pressed onto his person as to avoid south end turbulence.

"Hey, um, you two are going to want to see this."

38

"Chosen One"

Dammerung floated above the grave site. It wasn't an ornate mausoleum or complex tomb covered in jewels, just a single gravestone with a carving on it so faded it was difficult to make out, it was the crest of the Nomad Druids, who never were for ostentation, even in burial.

The sword rotated slowly over the grave, waiting for its owner, its friend, and the end of its journey. they stood before it in silence, feeling the end of the journey like a precipice, they just didn't know if at the bottom was a giant pillow, or a rusted nail pit.

"Kind of thought it was going to be some underground tomb with mazes and traps like Oman's" Ted said.

"Me too!" Carl added.

From the corner of his eye, Ted saw a second gravestone, just as simple as the first.

He walked up to it, Uli followed to get a better look, it had three words on it from an ancient language.

"Oman, what does it say?"

The Necromancer scanned the forgotten alphabet, "Roughly translated, Hillios, stupid ass horse."

"Oh yeah," Ted and Uli said in unison.

Uli went back to the sword that was pointing to the end of their quest, It was time for her to do what she chose to do.

She cracked her neck, took a good long look at her friends, the buzz she felt now was not of magic, it was from something else. Her and her faithful companions had gone through the strangest days of their lives. Now wanted by the law, hunted by monsters and what ever Mr. Sundae was, and almost being consumed by man-eating trees. Death was at their door, but here they are, at the end.

"Necromancer," Oman called Uli, "Go on now, do your undead duty." She chuckled and nodded.

She asked Carl for the dagger in her bag, Dammerung pulsing as if anticipating what Uli was planning, "Okay big boy, time to wake up your buddy."

She etched a circle around the grave to contain and focus the Eitherkreiss, a single prick of blood wasn't going to cut it, she slashed her palm startling the small group of witnesses. She stained the grave, then gripped the knife with her gashed hand and let the blood trickle down to the tip, making a constant drip of crimson to the foot of the grave.

"Time, space, causality, fate, here lies your chosen one, the destined but cut down."

The circle she had carved let out a burst of whitest flame, Ted felt the instinct to protect, but Carl gently grabbed his arm.

"Stay cool, she's just doing her thing."

"Let your friend do her duty," Oman added.

"I who am nothing have come to correct, to mend the broken strings of fate, I am a mere mortal. Wait, you know what? Fuck this ye olden time speak shit," Uli said.

"Listen you cosmic fuckwits, you dropped the ball and now some mortal is here to correct what your sorry asses couldn't. So are you going to let me fix this mess or not? Cause even if you don't help, I am gonna do it anyway."

The blood falling from Uli crystallized into crimson ice. The white flames dancing into a deep purple, morning sky grieving, whatever she was doing it was working, she turned to look at her travel band giving a thumbs up with her free hand, all (even Blood Fucker) returned a double thumbs up.

Her stomach felt like it dropped, gravity around them doubled. The black necromantic ooze ran from the corners of her lips. Magic pumped from the crystallized blood into the grave, the amount being pulled was immense, if she had tried such a thing yesterday she would have blacked out, foaming at the mouth, convulsing on the floor like a fumigated roach.

But she was working on a surplus. The army of the dead left her mind trashed like a perfect house party, but left her a gift of near limitless death magic.

"Now give me the words!" She screamed.

The gravestone shot out into the sky, boulders around them lifted off hovering in place as if spectators for what's to come.

The blood forest nearby screamed in jealousy at the surge of Eitherkreiss which it had no reach to feast on.

"Give me the words!" Dammerung shined ever brighter than the morning sun, a cyclone of energy spiraled up, bringing into its twist the purple and white energy that danced about.

The words appeared within her, each one as big and heavy

as mountains, they felt like they would squash her if she didn't spit them out.

"La dos Shikai!" The spiral of energy cut through the atmosphere into space, *"Vider Gen,"* The hard earth vibrating loose, the wind chime melody of Dammerung singing out loud enough to be heard all around Thira. Two words remained to be spoken.

"No!" Carl screamed, breaking Uli's concentration.

What felt like a dozen needles stabbed her, spear tips barely grazing her back, warm thick blood fell on her shoulders, She looked behind and saw Ted, eye clear, no guardian mode.

"Ted?"

He said nothing, three spears decorated his back, with one particularly large smoke spear clean through his right eye.

She could not scream, the light spiral above untwining.

Carl and Blood Fucker searched for the attacker behind and saw Mr. Sundae, half his face gone, body burnt to a crisp, teeth exposed and missing his nose, looking like a corpse mid incineration.

"Okay mother fuckers! Round two!"

Mr. Sundae readied a new volley of pikes, using the smoke coming off his own singed body as fuel.

"Ted, Ted! Ted no!" Uli said.

Ted managed a smile, "Nice to know your purpose, even for a moment."

Ted collapsed to the floor, dead before he hit the ground. The spears on his back and eye disappearing on impact.

Uli let out a magic boosted scream that cracked a line in the whole mesa.

Carl rushed a tackle to Mr. Sundae, but a burning fist to the face stopped his charge, he flew crashing into the floating boulders, falling off hitting the ground limp but breathing.

Blood Fucker shot into the sky belting out a full load of acid at Mr. Sundae, the fuming demigod blew the acid and the squirrel away, Blood Fucker meeting the same fate as Carl.

"We were having a fun time, but you little snot shits had to go and make it painful."

Black flames bursted from Uli's eyes, she broke her knife from the crystallized blood, she raised the dagger to the sky and with all her body dropped the knife into Ted's corpse.

"Uli no! You're splitting the spell in two!" cried Oman.

"VIDERGEN!"

"NO Uli!" But she did not listen.

"ULIMOTH!" she screamed, all sound in Thira disappeared. Mr. Sundae knowing this dance was about to end, produced a floating spear the size and girth of a light post.

His smoke poll sliced through the air, Uli closed her eyes, waiting for what looked like was going to be her very quick and very violent death.

She heard a hard *Pang!* As if a giant iron skillet parried the spear into space.

She opened her eyes and saw the spear stuck into a wall of floating mountain chunks.

Mr. Sundae produced a second spear double the size of the last, "Don't worry, Mr. Sundae don't miss twice." before he could launch it, what sounded like a quire of angels one million strong rushed him with a wall of sound.

An inhuman growl came from behind Uli, it could have

been a jet plane about to take flight.

"Ah shit," Mr. Sundae deadpanned, a concussive wave pushed everything not tethered to the floor, small tornadoes danced around the gravesite in chaotic glee.

"Uli, what's happening?" Ted breathed once more, the hole in his head gone, Uli went to the floor, hugging Ted tight enough to kill him again.

Standing over Mr. Sundae was Prince Aiden, seven feet tall, covered in his armor, looking as if he had been buried only last week. Dammerung sang in his right hand, sparks bursting from its edge as the dimension of light within rejoiced at their reunion.

"Well bless my bitches, ya did it, pleasure to meet a chosen one in person."

Mr. Sundae looked up at Aiden's gaunt face, his eyes not human, black as a well to hell. The growl coming from the revived chosen one was so deep, Mr. Sundae felt it shake his bones.

"You don't look very Chosen One at the moment, friend."

Mr. Sundae did not feel a holy aura, very much the opposite, it was menace with a need for destruction. Aiden let out a battle cry the equivalent of a planet of lions all roaring at once.

He broke Mr. Sundae's spear and summoned the full force of Dammerung to battle, every teeth cracking blow having the power of a light dimension behind it.

Reality warping with every attack, Mr. Sundae tried to escape time and time again, but Aiden's otherworldly power had its own gravitational pull, Mr. Sundae was pulled into the hurricane of sword slashes, the immortal felt like the end was near.

Humanity peaked out of Aiden's raged sunken eyes, he stopped his barrage at once. He looked around in confused panic.

"No, no, no, no, who did this?" he turned to Uli, "What have you done!?"

As if a gear broke loose in the universe, Aiden screamed towards the heavens.

Mr. Sundae with the last of his strength made his retreat, engulfing his body in his own smoke, puttering away like a poorly made rocket.

"The spell was split and diverted, it only half worked! That is not Aiden, it's a mindless abomination from a botched spell!" Oman said.

The maddened chosen one zeroed in on Uli and readied Dammerung, but his sanity poked out again from the frenzy."You fools, you've doomed everyone," Aiden wound up and launched his sword into heaven.

"You two! Look at me, it's all a lie, all of it, from the very start. Stop all this! I know you think you're doing the right thing but…" Aiden knelt, sticking his head out, "We've been played…" his final words cut short.

Twirling down like an incandescent saw blade, Dammerung came back down to earth decapitating his master, falling next to Aiden, both losing their incandescent glow.

39

"Stumped"

History felt dead set in repeating itself in regard to Aiden, this time allowing the prince to leave with some modicum of honor. Much like his first passing, all who were left standing in the now second failed attempt at the prophecy, were perplexed on what to do next, the chosen one's last words hanging heavy on every soul there.

"What the heck do we do now?" Carl asked.

Uli's brain had frozen, no thought entering or leaving.

Sacrifices made, family members lost, places of employment ruined, only for the shiny bastard to leave more questions on the pile, and then off himself, and for what?

Uli cycled the words "We've been played" over and over in her mind, what could have Aiden meant? The plan was sound, but the lack of the whole playbook on the greater machinations of Thira peaked its demonic head into the equation once more. Maybe the half revived hero was not sound of mind, maybe it was the last jumbled ramblings of a botched resurrection, or maybe Uli had to come to terms that she had doomed Thira, and she didn't even know how she did it, all she could do was imagine a giant read FAIL stamp brand her head multiple times.

"You saved me," Ted said, "You saved me Uli, you wasted a resurrection spell on me." Her ears twitched first, her eyes blinked second, she looked down to her revived buddy Ted.

"You saved me, but Aiden, what…"

Uli, with her eyes closed, smiled, "Well, he's not my bestie." The silence now was devoid of awkwardness. They may never kiss again, they may never be one in the fanciful frolics of romance, but the love each one had for the other in that moment was stronger than any bond existing in Thira.

And as Ted found his way up and embraced his pale witch of a companion, he felt something missing within, a phantom organ not present, a part of him misplaced, it was not a haunting or panicking sensation, but a raw wound of something taken.

Carl stood over Aiden's corpse, the hero's head a few steps away from the body. The only one worthy of wielding Etheria's light, gone for good now. It was faith that got Carl here, belief in a higher power, belief in his father, then at the end belief in his friends, now all three engines dead at the feet of the one man who could have validated all of it. Carl pondered the concept of this being in fact the lot in life for him and his new companions, winners only exist through the existence of losers, and only a few get to carry the gold. Or maybe it was just the light's turn to bend the knee, whatever the case it was a real bummer for everyone on that crumbling mesa. Perhaps trying was the original sin of the whole quest, them trying was in fact the mistake Aiden was warning them about. Prayer felt pointless, and Carl was now left with a whole aisle of his essence empty of faith.

Silence was in abundant supplies, allowing their minds to adjust to the new calibrations of the world, outside of them, a whole planet none the wiser of how close it was to change. Now the most pertinent truth being that their days were numbered, a bullseye painted on all of them, now just a waiting game for Volshtadt and company to come and eat them or whatever evil crap they did to enemies of the state.

"We can't leave him like this, the least we could do is put him back in his grave in peace." Carl said.

Uli and Ted knew it was the right thing to do, so they helped Carl give the fallen Hero one last proper burial.

Aiden had bursted out of the hard ground, leaving a crater easy enough to drag his larger than usual body back in, it took a couple of attempts to keep the head facing upward, but Uli locked it in place by shoving dirt around it like a poorly made defense wall on a sand castle.

"What do you think he meant? With that thing that we've been played?" Ted said.

"I have no idea, but it scares the living shit out of me." Uli said.

Oman moved his jaw to say something but opted not to, not now. Knowledge is power, and it could be volatile if shared at the wrong moment.

Ted and Carl picked Dammerung up, slowly walking it into the grave so it can finally be with its owner.

"STUMPED"

"At least it gets to finally be with its bud, that has to make this quest count for something right?" Ted said, trying to give Uli the participation trophy she didn't ask for.

"Yeah," She said, with a smile far sadder than any frown could compete with.

Carl gently wrapped Aiden's hands around Dammerung grip, making the whole visage look like one of those statues of ancient warriors in a museum.

None had caught it growing glow, all crawling out of the grave ready to push the gravel over Aiden. Uli caught it once she tossed her handful of rocks unceremoniously on the Chosen One's face.

Ted had a large boulder over his head, ready to chuck it in "Wait! Wait, wait, hold the phone, you see that?"

"See what?" Carl asked.

"The glow, it still has a little."

"Really let me see?" Carl checked. Ted, thoroughly ignored, decided to drop the boulder behind his back, the large rock scraping Ted's still naked ass to the point of needing disinfectant.

Dammerung ignited with its radiant beauty, the galaxies within it dancing once more. Ted's pain yet again, having its thunder stolen.

"Is he still alive?" wondered Carl.

They all looked at Aiden's head, mouth full of pebbles, his pupils pointing in different directions like a chameleon.

"Nope, still dead..." Uli said. The hero of fate limp in his tomb yet the sword still glowed on, it made no sense. Uli slid back in trying to get a better look at the anomaly, the only part of bare flesh touching the sword was Aiden's hands. She moved the fingers off Dammerung and the light went out, she placed them back and POW! The light was back.

She did this over and over, making the epileptic light show annoying to the rest of the party.

"Uli, please stop using the Chosen One like a cheap wedding light show," Carl said.

"From hand of chosen man, shall the Dammerung slay the Dark Lord's command? From hand of chosen man, shall the Dammerung slay the dark lord's command! From hand of chosen man shall the Dammerung slay the Dark Lord's command!!! Holy shit, fuck, fucking duck!" Uli sang in her ear poisoning tone.

"What? Explain yourself child, you're just repeating yourself like the town simpleton!" Oman said.

"The prophecy never said the chosen one had to be alive, it only really called for his hand if I remember right."

She gave none the ability to process her comment and went straight for her replica knife, Stabbing into Aiden's right forearm, sawing it off with manic enthusiasm. Horrified confusion was plastered on Ted, and Carl's face.

"You boys up for another road trip to the Capitol?" The only one who answered was Blood Fucker with an enthusiastic squeak.

40

"Panicked Room"

He had to have seen it now, the blast of Etherian light, The resurrection spiral that pierced the sky, the dimensional call of Dammerung, "It's done, it's done." Kalammet said to himself as he rushed to his King's quarters.

"Kalammet!" Volshtadt shouted from within his room.

Like a child who had done wrong and father finding out, Kalammet slowly opened the door. In the darkened room, smoke floated around the floor.

"My King, I can explain," Kalammet meekly said.

"No need."

Once the light of the hallway lit the room, Kalammet saw Mr. Sundae's neck crushed in Volshtadt's left hand, his smoke rushing into the angered President's eyes.

"I've been put up to speed with the situation."

"I see," Kalammet said, averting his eyes.

"You know what happens next?" Volshtadt said quietly. His hell blade Thigg rushing to its master's right grip.

"I do." Kalammet said, accepting his fate.

"Kneel and take my justice."

"No," Kalammet said, taking off his hood to show his ancient skin. Volshtadt's response was to unleash his Eitherkreiss aura in the room, red energy lashing out from his body.

"So be it," Volshtadt raised his sword to prepare an energy slash to off his creator, when the tip pointed to the ceiling Kalammet said one word.

"Auszeit."

The red energy stopped, Kalammet flipped the light switch on, erasing the menace from the room. Volshtadt stayed statue still with his sword raised high.

"My King, I do apologize, but when a child raises its hand at its father, discipline must be dealt."

Every muscle in his body refused command, Volshtadt's body was his no longer, stuck in his flesh prison, rage tripled on the already discovered betrayal, his purpose close to completion, now gone for good.

"Now, you and I are going to have a little chat." Kalammet said as he closed the door and made his way to an ornate recliner. Volshtadt's eyes bleeding white hot fury, all he was good for now was listening, and listen he will.

41

"Magic Cows"

Ogun felt her back spasm on the cold hard floor, the white artificial light burned her groggy bruised eyes. Her brain told her body to get up, but it took its time to commit to the request.

Her senses dull, but she could make out an annoying, head buzzing hum.

"Don't try to move fast there, you'll tip over and knock your head," an old voice said with the sweetest of tones to cut through the ancient rasp.

"Ya think they milked her on the way in?" asked a second senior citizen, this one sounding like he spent more time in a crop than a city block.

"I hate when you use that term, it doesn't feel right, makes it sound sexual."

"Sexual? Nobody said it was sexual, don't be gross now."

"Please say drain, or steal or something. Just not milking."

"Would both of you fine gentlemen please shut it?" Ogun already didn't like her situation, and being stuck with two bickering old folks did not help her mental peace one bit.

"Sorry Ogun, how's your head?" she managed to focus on the codger's face, she knew that voice from somewhere.

Bordering sixty, white hair to his ankles, built like a thin bamboo, the old guy smiled as he saw Ogun's grogginess give way to a small relieved smile.

"Reynald?" Ogun said.

"Yup, yup, yup, How long has it been hun?"

"That hot spring melding of the minds camping thing we did like ten years ago."

"That be the one yup, yup."

"The orgy at the end got wild! I always get a little uncomfortable when the druids start shape shifting?" said the second old timer.

Ogun looked over and saw a short rounded out man, bald and styling a golfing polo, wide shorts and flip flops. She knew the ancient pervert only by the name Ely.

"Ely," Ogun said, doing her best not to remember that golden years orgy she not only participated in but probably got the MVP award for.

"Where are we?" Ogun said, sounding like a hungover car crash survivor.

"Detention facility of some kind," Reynald pointed to the ceiling but mostly directed the attention to the whole of the building.

"Ya hear that annoying shit?" he tapped the hard steel floor with his heel.

"They pump a small electrical charge through the crap to keep a consistent dampening pulse."

Ogun raised an eyebrow, "Well shit, argonite?"

The mineral bane of the magical community was first

discovered in a volcano in the southern regions of Thira, that magma pit served as a sacrificial death pit by the local tribes, tossing in the wizard folk in order to appease their death god of the month.

"Yeah the whole place is made of it, guess they didn't want us blowing the place up."

"Hah! Blow," Ely laughed, despite the avalanche of eye rolls and groans, the tiny wizard was proud of his observational humor.

Ogun got the lay of the place, a long cathedral like corridor, comfy looking but tiny double beds were spread out in uniform rows. All ages and shapes of people sat and chatted. None looked like reanimated corpses, but there was a drained pale complexion to the general population of the wizard prison.

"This is where they've been collected then."

"Yup, yup, reeducation my middle nut," Reynald coughed out, "This is a fucking farm."

"Hence why the milking analogy plays man."

"Ely, please. They let out some gas to knock us out, they take three or four at a time, bring em back a couple of hours later a little lighter."

"They feed us three times a day, damn good food actually, the beds are comfy, open yard and jogging course, we even have a couple of Jacuzzi's."

"It be a pretty nice deal, if it wasn't for the two or three of us that turn to dust every week or so."

That last comment made Ogun sick to her stomach.

"Did a couple of weirdos in dragon costumes get you guys too?" Ogun asked.

"All of us. Who knew somebody got their hands on the

recipe for Drackenstat minions, fucking alchemists, messing it up for the rest of us." Reynald said.

"I gotta get out of here," Ogun said. Ely and Reynald snorted in retort.

"Words uttered by everyone in here at some point or another," Ely said, sounding serious for the first time since Ogun woke up.

"Y'all don't understand, something has come up, and it's gonna need everybody in this room to help out on it."

"What happened?"

Ogun gave a quick look to one of the corners, "I'll tell ya later, too many ears on the wall." They turned and saw literal ears popping out the argonite wall.

About the Author

Tony Merino is a creative writing teacher from San Antonio Texas. He takes care of his elderly parents as well as four dogs, and a cat.

He enjoys singing old anime intros, absorbing useless knowledge, and pretending to argue with people while driving to the grocery store.

Follow on Instagram.
@UNCHOSEN_BOOK

Book cover made by Cristina Franco.
@cristinafrancov

Made in the USA
Columbia, SC
01 February 2025